$\mathcal{V}$OICES OF THE $\mathcal{S}$OUTH

In the Land
of Dreamy Dreams

Short Fiction

Ellen Gilchrist

Louisiana State University Press

Baton Rouge

11 10 09 08 07 06 05 04 03 02
5 4 3 2 1

ISBN 0-8071-2829-5

I am grateful to the editors of the following journals, in whose pages some
of the stories in this volume originally appeared: *Prairie Schooner* for "The
President of the Louisiana Live Oak Society" and "Revenge," copyright ©
by the University of Nebraska Press; *New Orleans Review* for "Traveler"
and "The Famous Poll at Jody's Bar"; and *Intro 9* for "Rich."

This book was completed during a period of time when I was a Fellow of
The National Endowment for the Arts. I thank them for their faith and
support.

The paper in this book meets the guidelines for permanence and durability
of the Committee on Production Guidelines for Book Longevity of the
Council on Library Resources. ∞

For Rosalie and Freddy
who kept watch
and for Bill
who put me up to it

Contents

There's a Garden of Eden

Rich

Tom and Letty Wilson were rich in everything. They were rich in friends because Tom was a vice-president of the Whitney Bank of New Orleans and liked doing business with his friends, and because Letty was vice-president of the Junior League of New Orleans and had her picture in *Town and Country* every year at the Symphony Ball.

The Wilsons were rich in knowing exactly who they were because every year from Epiphany to Fat Tuesday they flew the beautiful green and gold and purple flag outside their house that meant that Letty had been queen of the Mardi Gras the year she was a debutante. Not that Letty was foolish enough to take the flag seriously.

Sometimes she was even embarrassed to call the yardman and ask him to come over and bring his high ladder.

"Preacher, can you come around on Tuesday and put up my flag?" she would ask.

"You know I can," the giant black man would answer. "I been saving time to put up your flag. I won't forget what a beautiful queen you made that year."

"Oh, hush, Preacher. I was a skinny little scared girl. It's a wonder I didn't fall off the balcony I was so scared. I'll see you on Monday." And Letty would think to herself what a big phony Preacher was and wonder when he was going to try to borrow some more money from them.

Tom Wilson considered himself a natural as a banker because he loved to gamble and wheel and deal. From the time he was a boy in a small Baptist town in Tennessee he had loved to play cards and match nickels and lay bets.

In high school he read *The Nashville Banner* avidly and kept an eye out for useful situations such as the lingering and suspenseful illnesses of Pope Pius.

3

"Let's get up a pool on the day the Pope will die," he would say to the football team, "I'll hold the bank." And because the Pope took a very long time to die with many close calls there were times when Tom was the richest left tackle in Franklin, Tennessee.

Tom had a favorite saying about money. He had read it in the *Reader's Digest* and attributed it to Andrew Carnegie. "Money," Tom would say, "is what you keep score with. Andrew Carnegie."

Another way Tom made money in high school was performing as an amateur magician at local birthday parties and civic events. He could pull a silver dollar or a Lucky Strike cigarette from an astonished six-year-old's ear or from his own left palm extract a seemingly endless stream of multicolored silk chiffon or cause an ordinary piece of clothesline to behave like an Indian cobra.

He got interested in magic during a convalescence from German measles in the sixth grade. He sent off for books of magic tricks and practiced for hours before his bedroom mirror, his quick clever smile flashing and his long fingers curling and uncurling from the sleeves of a black dinner jacket his mother had bought at a church bazaar and remade to fit him.

Tom's personality was too flamboyant for the conservative Whitney Bank, but he was cheerful and cooperative and when he made a mistake he had the ability to turn it into an anecdote.

"Hey, Fred," he would call to one of his bosses. "Come have lunch on me and I'll tell you a good one."

They would walk down St. Charles Avenue to where it crosses Canal and turns into Royal Street as it enters the French Quarter. They would walk into the crowded, humid excitement of the quarter, admiring the girls and watching the Yankee tourists sweat in their absurd spun-glass leisure suits, and turn into the side door of Antoine's or breeze past the maitre d' at Galatoire's or Brennan's.

When a red-faced waiter in funereal black had seated them at a choice table, Tom would loosen his Brooks Brothers' tie, turn his handsome brown eyes on his guest, and begin.

"That bunch of promoters from Dallas talked me into backing an idea to videotape all the historic sights in the quarter and rent the tapes to hotels to show on closed-circuit television. Goddamnit, Fred, I could just see those fucking tourists sitting around their hotel rooms on rainy days ordering from room service and taking in the Cabildo and the Presbytere on T.V." Tom laughed delightedly and waved his glass of vermouth at an elegantly dressed couple walking by the table.

"Well, they're barely breaking even on that one, and now they want to buy up a lot of soft porn movies and sell them to motels in Jefferson Parish. What do you think? Can we stay with them for a few more months?"

Then the waiter would bring them cold oysters on the half shell and steaming pompano *en papillote* and a wine steward would serve them a fine Meursault or a Piesporter, and Tom would listen to whatever advice he was given as though it were the most intelligent thing he had ever heard in his life.

Of course he would be thinking, "You stupid, impotent son of a bitch. You scrawny little frog bastard, I'll buy and sell you before it's over. I've got more brains in my balls than the whole snotty bunch of you."

"Tom, you always throw me off my diet," his friend would say, "damned if you don't."

"I told Letty the other day," Tom replied, "that she could just go right ahead and spend her life worrying about being buried in her wedding dress, but I didn't hustle my way to New Orleans all the way from north Tennessee to eat salads and melba toast. Pass me the French bread."

Letty fell in love with Tom the first time she laid eyes on him. He came to Tulane on a football scholarship and charmed his way into a fraternity of wealthy New Orleans boys famed for its drunkenness and its wild practical jokes. It was the same old story. Even the second, third, and fourth generation blue bloods of New Orleans need an infusion of new genes now and then.

The afternoon after Tom was initiated he arrived at the fraternity house with two Negro painters and sat in the low-hanging branches of a live oak tree overlooking Henry Clay Avenue directing them in painting an official-looking yellow-and-white-striped pattern on the street in front of the property. "D-R-U-N-K," he yelled to his painters, holding on to the enormous limb with one hand and pushing his black hair out of his eyes with the other. "Paint it to say D-R-U-N-K Z-O-N-E."

Letty stood near the tree with a group of friends watching him. He was wearing a blue shirt with the sleeves rolled up above his elbows, and a freshman beanie several sizes too small was perched on his head like a tipsy sparrow.

"I'm wearing this goddamn beanie forever," Tom yelled. "I'm wearing this beanie until someone brings me a beer," and Letty took the one she was holding and walked over to the tree and handed it to him.

One day a few weeks later, he commandeered a Bunny Bread truck while it was parked outside the fraternity house making a delivery. He picked up two friends and drove the truck madly around the Irish Channel, throwing fresh loaves of white and whole-wheat and rye bread to the astonished housewives.

"Steal from the rich, give to the poor," Tom yelled, and his companions gave up trying to reason with him and helped him yell.

"Free bread, free cake," they yelled, handing out powdered doughnuts and sweet rolls to a gang of kids playing baseball on a weed-covered vacant lot.

They stopped off at Darby's, an Irish bar where Tom made bets on races and football games, and took on some beer and left off some cinnamon rolls.

"Tom, you better go turn that truck in before they catch you," Darby advised, and Tom's friends agreed, so they drove the truck to the second-precinct police headquarters and turned themselves in. Tom used up half a year's allowance paying the damages, but it made his reputation.

In Tom's last year at Tulane a freshman drowned during a hazing accident at the Southern Yacht Club, and the event frightened Tom. He had never liked the boy and had suspected him of being involved with the queers and nigger lovers who hung around the philosophy department and the school newspaper. The boy had gone to prep school in the East and brought weird-looking girls to rush parties. Tom had resisted the temptation to blackball him as he was well connected in uptown society.

After the accident, Tom spent less time at the fraternity

house and more time with Letty, whose plain sweet looks and expensive clothes excited him.

"I can't go in the house without thinking about it," he said to Letty. "All we were doing was making them swim from pier to pier carrying martinis. I did it fifteen times the year I pledged."

"He should have told someone he couldn't swim very well," Letty answered. "It was an accident. Everyone knows it was an accident. It wasn't your fault." And Letty cuddled up close to him on the couch, breathing as softly as a cat.

Tom had long serious talks with Letty's mild, alcoholic father, who held a seat on the New York Stock Exchange, and in the spring of the year Tom and Letty were married in the Cathedral of Saint Paul with twelve bridesmaids, four flower girls, and seven hundred guests. It was pronounced a marriage made in heaven, and Letty's mother ordered masses said in Rome for their happiness.

They flew to New York on the way to Bermuda and spent their wedding night at the Sherry Netherland Hotel on Fifth Avenue. At least half a dozen of Letty's friends had lost their virginity at the same address, but the trip didn't seem prosaic to Letty.

She stayed in the bathroom a long time gazing at her plain face in the oval mirror and tugging at the white lace nightgown from the Lylian Shop, arranging it now to cover, now to reveal her small breasts. She crossed herself in the mirror, suddenly giggled, then walked out into the blue and gold bedroom as though she had been going to bed with men every night of her life. She had been up until three the night before reading a book on sexual intercourse. She offered her small unpainted mouth to Tom. Her pale hair smelled of Shalimar and carnations and candles. Now she was safe. Now life would begin.

"Oh, I love you, I love, I love, I love you," she whispered over and over. Tom's hands touching her seemed a strange and exciting passage that would carry her simple dreamy existence to a reality she had never encountered. She had never dreamed anyone so interesting would marry her.

Letty's enthusiasm and her frail body excited him, and he made love to her several times before he asked her to remove her gown.

7

The next day they breakfasted late and walked for a while along the avenue. In the afternoon Tom explained to his wife what her clitoris was and showed her some of the interesting things it was capable of generating, and before the day was out Letty became the first girl in her crowd to break the laws of God and the Napoleonic Code by indulging in oral intercourse.

Fourteen years went by and the Wilsons' luck held. Fourteen years is a long time to stay lucky even for rich people who don't cause trouble for anyone.

Of course, even among the rich there are endless challenges, unyielding limits, rivalry, envy, quirks of fortune. Letty's father grew increasingly incompetent and sold his seat on the exchange, and Letty's irresponsible brothers went to work throwing away the money in Las Vegas and L.A. and Zurich and Johannesburg and Paris and anywhere they could think of to fly to with their interminable strings of mistresses.

Tom envied them their careless, thoughtless lives and he was annoyed that they controlled their own money while Letty's was tied up in some mysterious trust, but he kept his thoughts to himself as he did his obsessive irritation over his growing obesity.

"Looks like you're putting on a little weight there," a friend would observe.

"Good, good," Tom would say, "makes me look like a man. I got a wife to look at if I want to see someone who's skinny."

He stayed busy gambling and hunting and fishing and being the life of the party at the endless round of dinners and cocktail parties and benefits and Mardi Gras functions that consume the lives of the Roman Catholic hierarchy that dominates the life of the city that care forgot.

Letty was preoccupied with the details of their domestic life and her work in the community. She took her committees seriously and actually believed that the work she did made a difference in the lives of other people.

The Wilsons grew rich in houses. They lived in a large Victorian house in the Garden District, and across Lake

Pontchartrain they had another Victorian house to stay in on the weekends, with a private beach surrounded by old moss-hung oak trees. Tom bought a duck camp in Plaquemines Parish and kept an apartment in the French Quarter in case one of his business friends fell in love with his secretary and needed someplace to be alone with her. Tom almost never used the apartment himself. He was rich in being satisfied to sleep with his own wife.

The Wilsons were rich in common sense. When five years of a good Catholic marriage went by and Letty inexplicably never became pregnant, they threw away their thermometers and ovulation charts and litmus paper and went down to the Catholic adoption agency and adopted a baby girl with curly black hair and hazel eyes. Everyone declared she looked exactly like Tom. The Wilsons named the little girl Helen and, as the months went by, everyone swore she even walked and talked like Tom.

At about the same time Helen came to be the Wilsons' little girl, Tom grew interested in raising Labrador retrievers. He had large wire runs with concrete floors built in the side yard for the dogs to stay in when he wasn't training them on the levee or at the park lagoon. He used all the latest methods for training Labs, including an electric cattle prod given to him by Chalin Perez himself and live ducks supplied by a friend on the Audubon Park Zoo Association Committee.

"Watch this, Helen," he would call to the little girl in the stroller, "watch this." And he would throw a duck into the lagoon with its secondary feathers neatly clipped on the left side and its feet tied loosely together, and one of the Labs would swim out into the water and carry it safely back and lay it at his feet.

As so often happens when childless couples are rich in common sense, before long Letty gave birth to a little boy, and then to twin boys, and finally to another little Wilson girl. The Wilsons became so rich in children the neighbors all lost count.

"Tom," Letty said, curling up close to him in the big walnut bed, "Tom, I want to talk to you about something important." The new baby girl was three months old. "Tom I want to talk to Father Delahoussaye and ask him if we can use some birth control. I think we have all the children we need for now."

Tom put his arms around her and squeezed her until he wrinkled her new green linen B. H. Wragge, and she screamed for mercy.

"Stop it," she said, "be serious. Do you think it's all right to do that?"

Then Tom agreed with her that they had had all the luck with children they needed for the present, and Letty made up her mind to call the cathedral and make an appointment. All her friends were getting dispensations so they would have time to do their work at the Symphony League and the Thrift Shop and the New Orleans Museum Association and the PTAs of the private schools.

All the Wilson children were in good health except Helen. The pediatricians and psychiatrists weren't certain what was wrong with Helen. Helen couldn't concentrate on anything. She didn't like to share and she went through stages of biting other children at the Academy of the Sacred Heart of Jesus.

The doctors decided it was a combination of prenatal brain damage and dyslexia, a complicated learning disability that is a fashionable problem with children in New Orleans.

Letty felt like she spent half her life sitting in offices talking to people about Helen. The office she sat in most often belonged to Dr. Zander. She sat there twisting her rings and avoiding looking at the box of Kleenex on Dr. Zander's desk. It made her feel like she was sleeping in a dirty bed even to think of plucking a Kleenex from Dr. Zander's container and crying in a place where strangers cried. She imagined his chair was filled all day with women weeping over terrible and sordid things like their husbands running off with their secretaries or their children not getting into the right clubs and colleges.

"I don't know what we're going to do with her next," Letty said. "If we let them hold her back a grade it's just going to make her more self-conscious than ever."

"I wish we knew about her genetic background. You people have pull with the sisters. Can't you find out?"

"Tom doesn't want to find out. He says we'll just be opening a can of worms. He gets embarrassed even talking about Helen's problem."

"Well," said Dr. Zander, crossing his short legs and settling his steel-rimmed glasses on his nose like a tiny bicycle stuck on a hill, "let's start her on Dexedrine."

So Letty and Dr. Zander and Dr. Mullins and Dr. Pickett and Dr. Smith decided to try an experiment. They decided to give Helen five milligrams of Dexedrine every day for twenty days each month, taking her off the drug for ten days in between.

"Children with dyslexia react to drugs strangely," Dr. Zander said. "If you give them tranquilizers it peps them up, but if you give them Ritalin or Dexedrine it calms them down and makes them able to think straight."

"You may have to keep her home and have her tutored on the days she is off the drug," he continued, "but the rest of the time she should be easier to live with." And he reached over and patted Letty on the leg and for a moment she thought it might all turn out all right after all.

Helen stood by herself on the playground of the beautiful old pink-brick convent with its drooping wrought-iron balconies covered with ficus. She was watching the girl she liked talking with some other girls who were playing jacks. All the little girls wore blue-and-red-plaid skirts and navy blazers or sweaters. They looked like a disorderly marching band. Helen was waiting for the girl, whose name was Lisa, to decide if she wanted to go home with her after school and spend the afternoon. Lisa's mother was divorced and worked downtown in a department store, so Lisa rode the streetcar back and forth from school and could go anywhere she liked until 5:30 in the afternoon. Sometimes she went home with Helen so she wouldn't have to ride the streetcar. Then Helen would be so excited the hours until school let out would seem to last forever.

Sometimes Lisa liked her and wanted to go home with her and other times she didn't, but she was always nice to Helen and let her stand next to her in lines.

Helen watched Lisa walking toward her. Lisa's skirt was two inches shorter than those of any of the other girls, and

11

she wore high white socks that made her look like a skater. She wore a silver identification bracelet and Revlon nail polish.

"I'll go home with you if you get your mother to take us to get an Icee," Lisa said. "I was going last night but my mother's boyfriend didn't show up until after the place closed so I was going to walk to Manny's after school. Is that O.K.?"

"I think she will," Helen said, her eyes shining. "I'll go call her up and see."

"Naw, let's just go swing. We can ask her when she comes." Then Helen walked with her friend over to the swings and tried to be patient waiting for her turn.

The Dexedrine helped Helen concentrate and it helped her get along better with other people, but it seemed to have an unusual side effect. Helen was chubby and Dr. Zander had led the Wilsons to believe the drug would help her lose weight, but instead she grew even fatter. The Wilsons were afraid to force her to stop eating for fear they would make her nervous, so they tried to reason with her.

"Why can't I have any ice cream?" she would say. "Daddy is fat and he eats all the ice cream he wants." She was leaning up against Letty, stroking her arm and petting the baby with her other hand. They were in an upstairs sitting room with the afternoon sun streaming in through the French windows. Everything in the room was decorated with different shades of blue, and the curtains were white with old-fashioned blue-and-white-checked ruffles.

"You can have ice cream this evening after dinner," Letty said, "I just want you to wait a few hours before you have it. Won't you do that for me?"

"Can I hold the baby for a while?" Helen asked, and Letty allowed her to sit in the rocker and hold the baby and rock it furiously back and forth crooning to it.

"Is Jennifer beautiful, Mother?" Helen asked.

"She's O.K., but she doesn't have curly black hair like you. She just has plain brown hair. Don't you see, Helen, that's why we want you to stop eating between meals, because you're so pretty and we don't want you to get too fat. Why don't you go outside and play with Tim and not try to think about ice cream so much?"

"I don't care," Helen said, "I'm only nine years old and I'm hungry. I want you to tell the maids to give me some ice cream now," and she handed the baby to her mother and ran out of the room.

The Wilsons were rich in maids, and that was a good thing because there were all those children to be taken care of and cooked for and cleaned up after. The maids didn't mind taking care of the Wilson children all day. The Wilsons' house was much more comfortable than the ones they lived in, and no one cared whether they worked very hard or not as long as they showed up on time so Letty could get to her meetings. The maids left their own children with relatives or at home watching television, and when they went home at night they liked them much better than if they had spent the whole day with them.

The Wilson house had a wide white porch across the front and down both sides. It was shaded by enormous oak trees and furnished with swings and wicker rockers. In the afternoons the maids would sit on the porch and other maids from around the neighborhood would come up pushing prams and strollers and the children would all play together on the porch and in the yard. Sometimes the maids fixed lemonade and the children would sell it to passersby from a little stand.

The maids hated Helen. They didn't care whether she had dyslexia or not. All they knew was that she was a lot of trouble to take care of. One minute she would be as sweet as pie and cuddle up to them and say she loved them and the next minute she wouldn't do anything they told her.

"You're a nigger, nigger, nigger, and my mother said I could cross St. Charles Avenue if I wanted to," Helen would say, and the maids would hold their lips together and look into each other's eyes.

One afternoon the Wilson children and their maids were sitting on the porch after school with some of the neighbors' children and maids. The baby was on the porch in a bassinet on wheels and a new maid was looking out for her. Helen was in the biggest swing and was swinging as high as she could go so that none of the other children could get in the swing with her.

"Helen," the new maid said, "it's Tim's turn in the swing. You been swinging for fifteen minutes while Tim's been waiting. You be a good girl now and let Tim have a turn. You too big to act like that."

"You're just a high yeller nigger," Helen called, "and you can't make me do anything." And she swung up higher and higher.

This maid had never had Helen call her names before and she had a quick temper and didn't put up with children calling her a nigger. She walked over to the swing and grabbed the chain and stopped it from moving.

"You say you're sorry for that, little fat honky white girl," she said, and made as if to grab Helen by the arms, but Helen got away and started running, calling over her shoulder, "Nigger, can't make me do anything."

She was running and looking over her shoulder and she hit the bassinet and it went rolling down the brick stairs so fast none of the maids or children could stop it. It rolled down the stairs and threw the baby onto the sidewalk and the blood from the baby's head began to move all over the concrete like a little ruby lake.

The Wilsons' house was on Philip Street, a street so rich it even had its own drugstore. Not some tacky chain drugstore with everything on special all the time, but a cute drugstore made out of a frame bungalow with gingerbread trim. Everything inside cost twice as much as it did in a regular drugstore, and the grown people could order any kind of drugs they needed and a green Mazda pickup would bring them right over. The children had to get their drugs from a fourteen-year-old pusher in Audubon Park named Leroi, but they could get all the ice cream and candy and chewing gum they wanted from the drugstore and charge it to their parents.

No white adults were at home in the houses where the maids worked so they sent the children running to the drugstore to bring the druggist to help with the baby. They called the hospital and ordered an ambulance and they called several doctors and they called Tom's bank. All the children who were old enough ran to the drugstore except Helen. Helen sat on the porch steps staring down at the baby with the maids hovering over it like swans, and she was crying and screaming and beating her hands against her head. She was in one of the periods when she couldn't have Dexedrine. She screamed and screamed, but none of the maids had time to help her. They were too busy with the baby.

"Shut up, Helen," one of the maids called. "Shut up that goddamn screaming. This baby is about to die."

A police car and the local patrol service drove up. An ambulance arrived and the yard filled with people. The druggist and one of the maids rode off in the ambulance with the baby. The crowd in the yard swarmed and milled and swam before Helen's eyes like a parade.

Finally they stopped looking like people and just looked like spots of color on the yard. Helen ran up the stairs and climbed under her cherry four-poster bed and pulled her pillows and her eiderdown comforter under it with her. There were cereal boxes and an empty ice cream carton and half a tin of English cookies under the headboard. Helen was soaked with sweat and her little Lily playsuit was tight under the arms and cut into her flesh. Helen rolled up in the comforter and began to dream the dream of the heavy clouds. She dreamed she was praying, but the beads of the rosary slipped through her fingers so quickly she couldn't catch them and it was cold in the church and beautiful and fragrant, then dark, then light, and Helen was rolling in the heavy clouds that rolled her like biscuit dough. Just as she was about to suffocate they rolled her face up to the blue air above the clouds. Then Helen was a pink kite floating above the houses at evening. In the yards children were playing and fathers were driving up and baseball games were beginning and the sky turned gray and closed upon the city like a lid.

And now the baby is alone with Helen in her room and the door is locked and Helen ties the baby to the table so it won't fall off.

"Hold still, Baby, this will just be a little shot. This won't hurt much. This won't take a minute." And the baby is still and Helen begins to work on it.

Letty knelt down beside the bed. "Helen, please come out from under there. No one is mad at you. Please come out and help me, Helen. I need you to help me."

Helen held on tighter to the slats of the bed and squeezed her eyes shut and refused to look at Letty.

Letty climbed under the bed to touch the child. Letty was crying and her heart had an anchor in it that kept digging in and sinking deeper and deeper.

Dr. Zander came into the bedroom and knelt beside the bed and began to talk to Helen. Finally he gave up being reasonable and wiggled his small gray-suited body under the bed and Helen was lost in the area of arms that tried to hold her.

Tom was sitting in the bank president's office trying not to let Mr. Saunders know how much he despised him or how much it hurt and mattered to him to be listening to a lecture. Tom thought he was too old to have to listen to lectures. He was tired and he wanted a drink and he wanted to punch the bastard in the face.

"I know, I know," he answered, "I can take care of it. Just give me a month or two. You're right. I'll take care of it."

And he smoothed the pants of his cord suit and waited for the rest of the lecture.

A man came into the room without knocking. Tom's secretary was behind him.

"Tom, I think your baby has had an accident. I don't know any details. Look, I've called for a car. Let me go with you."

Tom ran up the steps of his house and into the hallway full of neighbors and relatives. A girl in a tennis dress touched him on the arm, someone handed him a drink. He ran up the winding stairs to Helen's room. He stood in the doorway. He could see Letty's shoes sticking out from under the bed. He could hear Dr. Zander talking. He couldn't go near them.

"Letty," he called, "Letty, come here, my god, come out from there."

No one came to the funeral but the family. Letty wore a plain dress she would wear any day and the children all wore their school clothes.

The funeral was terrible for the Wilsons, but afterward they went home and all the people from the Garden District and from all over town started coming over to cheer them up. It looked like the biggest cocktail party ever held in New

Orleans. It took four rented butlers just to serve the drinks. Everyone wanted to get in on the Wilsons' tragedy.

In the months that followed the funeral Tom began to have sinus headaches for the first time in years. He was drinking a lot and smoking again. He was allergic to whiskey, and when he woke up in the morning his nose and head were so full of phlegm he had to vomit before he could think straight.

He began to have trouble with his vision.

One November day the high yellow windows of the Shell Oil Building all turned their eyes upon him as he stopped at the corner of Poydras and Carondelet to wait for a streetlight, and he had to pull the car over to a curb and talk to himself for several minutes before he could drive on.

He got back all the keys to his apartment so he could go there and be alone and think. One afternoon he left work at two o'clock and drove around Jefferson Parish all afternoon drinking Scotch and eating potato chips.

Not as many people at the bank wanted to go out to lunch with him anymore. They were sick and tired of pretending his expensive mistakes were jokes.

One night Tom was gambling at the Pickwick Club with a poker group and a man jokingly accused him of cheating. Tom jumped up from the table, grabbed the man and began hitting him with his fists. He hit the man in the mouth and knocked out his new gold inlays.

"You dirty little goddamn bond peddler, you son of a bitch! I'll kill you for that," Tom yelled, and it took four waiters to hold him while the terrified man made his escape. The next morning Tom resigned from the club.

He started riding the streetcar downtown to work so he wouldn't have to worry about driving his car home if he got drunk. He was worrying about money and he was worrying about his gambling debts, but most of the time he was thinking about Helen. She looked so much like him that he believed people would think she was his illegitimate child. The more he tried to talk himself into believing the baby's death was an accident, the more obstinate his mind became.

The Wilson children were forbidden to take the Labs out of the kennels without permission. One afternoon Tom came home earlier than usual and found Helen sitting in the open door of one of the kennels playing with a half-grown litter of puppies. She was holding one of the puppies and the others were climbing all around her and spilling out onto the grass. She held the puppy by its forelegs, making it dance in the air, then letting it drop. Then she would gather it in her arms and hold it tight and sing to it.

Tom walked over to the kennel and grabbed her by an arm and began to paddle her as hard as he could.

"Goddamn you, what are you trying to do? You know you aren't supposed to touch those dogs. What in the hell do you think you're doing?"

Helen was too terrified to scream. The Wilsons never spanked their children for anything.

"I didn't do anything to it. I was playing with it," she sobbed.

Letty and the twins came running out of the house and when Tom saw Letty he stopped hitting Helen and walked in through the kitchen door and up the stairs to the bedroom. Letty gave the children to the cook and followed him.

Tom stood by the bedroom window trying to think of something to say to Letty. He kept his back turned to her and he was making a nickel disappear with his left hand. He thought of himself at Tommie Keenen's birthday party wearing his black coat and hat and doing his famous rope trick. Mr. Keenen had given him fifteen dollars. He remembered sticking the money in his billfold.

"My god, Letty, I'm sorry. I don't know what the shit's going on. I thought she was hurting the dog. I know I shouldn't have hit her and there's something I need to tell you about the bank. Kennington is getting sacked. I may be part of the housecleaning."

"Why didn't you tell me before? Can't Daddy do anything?"

"I don't want him to do anything. Even if it happens it doesn't have anything to do with me. It's just bank politics. We'll say I quit. I want to get out of there anyway. That fucking place is driving me crazy."

Tom put the nickel in his pocket and closed the bedroom door. He could hear the maid down the hall comforting Helen. He didn't give a fuck if she cried all night. He walked over to Letty and put his arms around her. He smelled like

18

he'd been drinking for a week. He reached under her dress and pulled down her pantyhose and her underpants and began kissing her face and hair while she stood awkwardly with the pants and hose around her feet like a halter. She was trying to cooperate.

She forgot that Tom smelled like sweat and whiskey. She was thinking about the night they were married. Every time they made love Letty pretended it was that night. She had spent thousands of nights in a bridal suite at the Sherry Netherland Hotel in New York City.

Letty lay on the walnut bed leaning into a pile of satin pillows and twisting a gold bracelet around her wrist. She could hear the children playing outside. She had a headache and her stomach was queasy, but she was afraid to take a Valium or an aspirin. She was waiting for the doctor to call her back and tell her if she was pregnant. She already knew what he was going to say.

Tom came into the room and sat by her on the bed.

"What's wrong?"

"Nothing's wrong. Please don't do that. I'm tired."

"Something's wrong."

"Nothing's wrong. Tom, please leave me alone."

Tom walked out through the French windows and onto a little balcony that overlooked the play yard and the dog runs. Sunshine flooded Philip Street, covering the houses and trees and dogs and children with a million volts a minute. It flowed down to hide in the roots of trees, glistening on the cars, baking the street, and lighting Helen's rumpled hair where she stooped over the puppy. She was singing a little song. She had made up the song she was singing.

"The baby's dead. The baby's dead. The baby's gone to heaven."

"Jesus God," Tom muttered. All up and down Philip Street fathers were returning home from work. A jeep filled with teenagers came tearing past and threw a beer can against the curb.

Six or seven pieces of Tom's mind sailed out across the street and stationed themselves along the power line that zigzagged back and forth along Philip Street between the live oak trees.

The pieces of his mind sat upon the power line like a row of black starlings. They looked him over.

Helen took the dog out of the buggy and dragged it over to the kennel.

"Jesus Christ," Tom said, and the pieces of his mind flew back to him as swiftly as they had flown away and entered his eyes and ears and nostrils and arranged themselves in their proper places like parts of a phrenological head.

Tom looked at his watch. It said 6:15. He stepped back into the bedroom and closed the French windows. A vase of huge roses from the garden hid Letty's reflection in the mirror.

"I'm going to the camp for the night. I need to get away. Besides, the season's almost over."

"All right," Letty answered. "Who are you going with?"

"I think I'll take Helen with me. I haven't paid any attention to her for weeks."

"That's good," Letty said, "I really think I'm getting a cold. I'll have a tray up for supper and try to get some sleep."

Tom moved around the room, opening drawers and closets and throwing some gear into a canvas duffel bag. He changed into his hunting clothes.

He removed the guns he needed from a shelf in the upstairs den and cleaned them neatly and thoroughly and zipped them into their carriers.

"Helen," he called from the downstairs porch. "Bring the dog in the house and come get on some play clothes. I'm going to take you to the duck camp with me. You can take the dog."

"Can we stop and get beignets?" Helen called back, coming running at the invitation.

"Sure we can, honey. Whatever you like. Go get packed. We'll leave as soon as dinner is over."

It was past 9:00 at night. They crossed the Mississippi River from the New Orleans side on the last ferry going to Algier's Point. There was an offshore breeze and a light rain fell on the old brown river. The Mississippi River smelled like the inside of a nigger cabin, powerful and fecund. The smell came in Tom's mouth until he felt he could chew it.

He leaned over the railing and vomited. He felt better and

walked back to the red Chevrolet pickup he had given himself for a birthday present. He thought it was chic for a banker to own a pickup.

Helen was playing with the dog, pushing him off the seat and laughing when he climbed back on her lap. She had a paper bag of doughnuts from the French Market and was eating them and licking the powdered sugar from her fingers and knocking the dog off the seat.

She wasn't the least bit sleepy.

"I'm glad Tim didn't get to go. Tim was bad at school, that's why he had to stay home, isn't it? The sisters called Momma. I don't like Tim. I'm glad I got to go by myself." She stuck her fat arms out the window and rubbed Tom's canvas hunting jacket. "This coat feels hard. It's all dirty. Can we go up in the cabin and talk to the pilot?"

"Sit still, Helen."

"Put the dog in the back, he's bothering me." She bounced up and down on the seat. "We're going to the duck camp. We're going to the duck camp."

The ferry docked. Tom drove the pickup onto the blacktop road past the city dump and on into Plaquemines Parish.

They drove into the brackish marshes that fringe the Gulf of Mexico where it extends in ragged fingers along the coast below and to the east of New Orleans. As they drove closer to the sea the hardwoods turned to palmetto and water oak and willow.

The marshes were silent. Tom could smell the glasswort and black mangrove, the oyster and shrimp boats.

He wondered if it were true that children and dogs could penetrate a man's concealment, could know him utterly.

Helen leaned against his coat and prattled on.

In the Wilson house on Philip Street Tim and the twins were cuddled up by Letty, hearing one last story before they went to bed.

A blue wicker tray held the remains of the children's hot chocolate. The china cups were a confirmation present sent to Letty from Limoges, France.

Now she was finishing reading a wonderful story by Ludwig Bemelmans about a little convent girl in Paris named

Madeline who reforms the son of the Spanish ambassador, putting an end to his terrible habit of beheading chickens on a miniature guillotine.

Letty was feeling better. She had decided God was just trying to make up to her for Jennifer.

The camp was a three-room wooden shack built on pilings out over Bayou Lafouche, which runs through the middle of the parish.

The inside of the camp was casually furnished with old leather office furniture, hand-me-down tables and lamps, and a walnut poker table from Neiman-Marcus. Photographs of hunts and parties were tacked around the walls. Over the poker table were pictures of racehorses and their owners and an assortment of ribbons won in races.

Tom laid the guns down on the bar and opened a cabinet over the sink in the part of the room that served as a kitchen. The nigger hadn't come to clean up after the last party and the sink was piled with half-washed dishes. He found a clean glass and a bottle of Tanqueray gin and sat down behind the bar.

Helen was across the room on the floor finishing the beignets and trying to coax the dog to come closer. He was considering it. No one had remembered to feed him.

Tom pulled a new deck of cards out of a drawer, broke the seal, and began to shuffle them.

Helen came and stood by the bar. "Show me a trick, Daddy. Make the queen disappear. Show me how to do it."

"Do you promise not to tell anyone the secret? A magician never tells his secrets."

"I won't tell. Daddy, please show me, show me now."

Tom spread out the cards. He began to explain the trick.

"All right, you go here and here, then here. Then pick up these in just the right order, but look at the people while you do it, not at the cards."

"I'm going to do it for Lisa."

"She's going to beg you to tell the secret. What will you do then?"

"I'll tell her a magician never tells his secrets."

Tom drank the gin and poured some more.

"Now let me do it to you, Daddy."

22

"Not yet, Helen. Go sit over there with the dog and practice it where I can't see what you're doing. I'll pretend I'm Lisa and don't know what's going on."

Tom picked up the Kliengunther 7 mm. magnum rifle and shot the dog first, splattering its brains all over the door and walls. Without pausing, without giving her time to raise her eyes from the red and gray and black rainbow of the dog, he shot the little girl.

The bullet entered her head from the back. Her thick body rolled across the hardwood floor and lodged against a hat rack from Jody Mellon's old office in the Hibernia Bank Building. One of her arms landed on a pile of old *Penthouse* magazines and her disordered brain flung its roses north and east and south and west and rejoined the order from which it casually arose.

Tom put down the rifle, took a drink of the thick gin, and, carrying the pistol, walked out onto the pier through the kitchen door. Without removing his glasses or his hunting cap he stuck the .38 Smith and Wesson revolver against his palate and splattered his own head all over the new pier and the canvas covering of the Boston Whaler. His body struck the boat going down and landed in eight feet of water beside a broken crab trap left over from the summer.

A pair of deputies from the Plaquemines Parish sheriff's office found the bodies.

Everyone believed it was some terrible inexplicable mistake or accident.

No one believed that much bad luck could happen to a nice lady like Letty Dufrechou Wilson, who never hurt a flea or gave anyone a minute's trouble in her life.

No one believed that much bad luck could get together between the fifteenth week after Pentecost and the third week in Advent.

No one believed a man would kill his own little illegitimate dyslexic daughter just because she was crazy.

And no one, not even the district attorney of New Orleans, wanted to believe a man would shoot a $3,000 Labrador retriever sired by Super Chief out of Prestidigitation.

The President of the
Louisiana Live Oak Society

The spring that Robert McLaurin was fourteen he had a black friend named Gus who lived underneath a huge live oak tree in Audubon Park. It was a tree so old and imposing that people in New Orleans called it the President of the Louisiana Live Oak Society.

Gus had a regular home somewhere inside the St. Thomas Street project, with a mother and brothers and sisters, but for all practical purposes he lived underneath the two-hundred-year-old tree in front of Dr. Alton Ochsner's palatial stucco house on Exposition Boulevard.

Imagine a brilliant day in early spring. It is the middle of the afternoon and under the low-hanging branches of the oak tree the air is quiet and cool and smells of all the gardens on the boulevard; confederate jasmine, honeysuckle, sweet alyssum, magnolia, every stereotyped southern flower you can imagine has mingled its individual odor into an ardent humid soup.

In the distance traffic is going along the avenue and a snatch of music floats across the street from the conservatory at Loyola University.

There is room under the tree for twenty or thirty kids on a good day. It is a perfect office for the youngest and most successful dope pushers on the river side of St. Charles Avenue.

Those spring afternoons of 1971 Robert would cut his last-period physical education class and come riding up on his bike playing his portable radio at full volume. Station

24

WTIX would be playing a love song by Judy Collins or "American Pie" by Don McLean, the national anthem of 1971.

Gus would be curled up asleep in the roots of the tree. From a distance he looked like an old catcher's mitt. He wore the same thing every day, a brown leather flight jacket and a pair of indefinite-colored plaid pants so worn that the lines of the plaid all ran together at the edges.

"You got any money?" Gus would ask, rubbing the sleep from his eyes with a dirty fist.

"Yeah, I got plenty. Last week they gave me twenty dollars to buy a track suit with. You want to get a mufflelata?"

"Let's smoke first."

Then Gus would open his cigar box, carefully remove a paper from its folder, pour the beautifully manicured dope onto the paper and roll it into a thin cylinder. He was careful, keeping his back to the wind if there was any so as not to spill a piece. He performed his ceremony to perfection, the rank aroma of his slept-in clothes rising to meet the spectacular smell of the marijuana as he lit the joint with dignity and passed it to Robert.

"How much stuff we got?" Robert asked.

"Not much. We got to find Uncle Clarence and hit him up. We hardly got enough for everyone that's coming today."

Roman Catholic girls in plaid uniform skirts rode by on bikes, their legs flashing in the sunlight.

"You know many of them Catholic girls?" Gus asked, making conversation.

"Yeah, I know them, but they don't talk to me. They're pretty stuck-up."

"How come?" Gus said.

"They go out with older guys. See that one over there," and he pointed out Darlene Trilling, riding by on a ten-speed; "she's really Jewish. She loves a senior in high school but her parents won't let her go out with him. She lives next door to me. She's probably going off somewhere to meet him right this minute."

"How come they won't let her?" Gus asked.

"They're probably afraid he'll give her some dope or something."

Gus started laughing his famous laugh. His face lit up like a three-tiered chandelier. He didn't hold anything back when he laughed.

"You should have seen my momma last Saturday," he said. "She outran a black cop. He couldn't catch her for anything and he knows that block as good as she does. She's fast as lightning. I'm fast like her."

"Is she a big woman?" Robert asked politely.

"Naw, she's little like me. One time when I got sick she put me in her nightgown. It just fit."

The oak tree held the boys like a spell. They rolled another joint.

"Someday I'll get a Buick and deal out of it," Gus said.

"What if they make dope legal?"

Gus looked scared. He looked like Robert had suggested they were going to drop a bomb on the park that very afternoon.

"They can't make it legal. The bars won't let them. It would run all the bars out of business."

They smoked in peace, talking about cars.

"Let's go get a mufflelata before the other kids get here," Robert said, stretching and getting up.

Gus hopped on the handlebars of Robert's bike and they rode off to Tranchina's, an Italian restaurant on Magazine Street that sells mufflelata sandwiches to go. A mufflelata is a plate-sized loaf of wop bread piled high with salami, bologna, pepperoni, mozzarella cheese, and soaked with olive salad. Gus and Robert ate out frequently that spring and this was one of their favorite meals.

"I wish we could get a cold beer to go with the mufflelata."

"There's no place will sell us one. I'll steal some out of the refrigerator for tomorrow."

"What about Darby's, the bookie?"

"Naw, he won't take a chance just to sell a couple of beers."

"Well, we can get an Icee at the Tote-Sum store."

A baby-blue Lincoln Continental turned the corner by the Chandlers' white picket fence and nearly ran over them. They were stoned, riding along looking at the red-and-pink azaleas and didn't see it coming. Gus managed to jump free and landed on his feet still holding the cigar box.

"Robert!" It was his mother. She had just come from the beauty parlor and her hair looked like a helmet for the Los Angeles Rams.

"Robert, come here to me." She pulled his head into the car window. "What are you doing with that black boy?" Robert's mother was a liberal. She never called black people niggers or Negroes even when she was mad at them.

"He's just a kid. I was giving him a ride to the Tote-Sum."

"Why aren't you at practice?" Her helmet moved up and down as she talked.

"They canceled it. The coach is sick. Listen, you almost ran over us, do you know that?" He had her on the defensive. She was very sensitive about her driving.

"Robert, I'm on my way to the grocery. You be home at six."

She drove off wearing her philosophical look. Jean-Paul Sartre couldn't have done it better.

"That was my mother."

"You scared of her?"

"God no. She's scared of me. She's afraid I'll die like my brother. He died when he was four. He had something wrong with him when he was born."

"Only person I'm scared of is my mother. She'll beat the daylights out of me if she finds out I'm dealing. My cousin just got put in jail for dealing. They put him in the House of D for a week."

"The what?"

"The House of D. The House of Detention. It's supposed to be for over eighteen and he ain't but sixteen but that's where he is and he cries every time they talk to him. Somebody stole his towel the first day he was there."

They ate the mufflelata and drank an Icee and rode back to the park and sold the rest of their stuff. Then they decided to ride down to the project and look for Uncle Clarence.

Supplies were a problem. They tried raising a crop on the back side of the levee, but the cops dug it up. They managed to bring in a small crop in Robert's grandmother's backyard while she was on a tour of Scandinavia with her bridge club, but that was a one-shot deal.

They started off for the project. They rode down Tchoupitoulas Street, which runs in a crescent along the levee lined with wharves and warehouses.

It was supposed to be dangerous to go into the project, but from Robert's elevated point of view the project just looked like a lot of old brick apartment buildings with iron balconies hanging off the sides like abandoned birds' nests and aluminum foil on half the windows to keep out the heat.

It was late afternoon and people were sitting on the stoops talking and drinking beer. Some kids were having a war with Coke bottles full of muddy water for ammunition. Robert and Gus went up a flight of stairs in one of the buildings and Gus's oldest sister met them at the door. She was taller and lighter than Gus, dressed in a ruffled white shirt and a short blue skirt.

"Where you think you been?" she demanded. Robert could smell her cool perfume.

"I been out on business," Gus said. "Where's momma?"

"She's gone to the store and you better stay here till she gets back. She sent Uncle Clarence looking for you yesterday."

She gave Robert a haughty look and settled back on the sofa where she was polishing her fingernails and watching a movie on television. She was studying to be a secretary.

The apartment was small and crowded with furniture. In one corner was a brass coatrack with ten or twelve different colored coats on it. It looked like a melted carousel. Robert kept staring at it, pulling in his pupils to make it look weirder and weirder.

"What's wrong with him?" Gus's sister demanded, pointing a newly coated nail at Robert.

"That's Robert. He does business with me uptown. There ain't nothing wrong with him some food won't fix. Where's Uncle Clarence now. You seen him?"

"He's probably still looking for you."

Gus liked to eat all the time when he was high. He made some peanut-butter sandwiches and they went off looking for his uncle.

They found Clarence sitting on the steps of a neighboring building drinking Apple Jack wine and flirting with a girlfriend. He was light-complected and wore a mustache and a carefully ironed African Mau-Mau shirt.

"Good evening," Gus smiled politely at the lady. "Uncle Clarence, you been looking for me?"

"Come here, Gus," Clarence said and pulled the boys out of earshot of the lady. "Gus, you got me in all kinds of trouble with your momma. She yelled at me for an hour yesterday. What you been doing with that stuff, smoking it yourself?"

"No, I ain't. This here is my partner, Robert. We don't do nothing but sell it to rich white kids in the park. Robert lets me keep supplies in his basement when we got anything to keep. And I got the money I owe you too." Gus produced three ten dollar bills and some crumpled ones and started counting it out to his uncle.

"Well, you ain't getting any more shit off me one way or the other." Clarence was feeling good. He had drunk just the right amount of Apple Jack. He kept his hand on the boy's shoulder as he talked. "I don't feel like having your momma after me and I'm off you for laying out so much. That's what's got her so hot."

"Uncle Clarence, you can't do me this way. I got my partner, I got my business, I got my customers. Momma ain't gonna find out anything. I'll stay home every night. I never knew you to be so scared of her before."

Gus was pulling out all the stops. Great tears were forming in the corners of his eyes.

"Oh, for Jesus' sake," Clarence said, not wanting the lady to see him making a kid cry. "I'll give you enough for one more week and we'll see how you stay home and keep her pacified. You come over to my place after dinner and I'll fix you up."

Gus and Robert looked at each other. Their eyes lit up like someone had just dropped a quarter in a pinball machine. They were set for another week.

Robert McLaurin's father, his name was Will, thought the spring of 1971 was the worst time he had ever lived through. He was a management lawyer. All he did at work was try Equal Opportunity Employment cases, and he had lost five in a row. All he did at home was argue with Robert McLaurin's mother, her name was Lelia, about whether or not Robert was taking drugs.

They argued so much about Robert they had stopped being in love with each other. All day long at the office Will thought about the argument from the day before and used his legal mind to think up ways to make his arguments more convincing.

He would drive up in front of his house after work and sometimes it would take him three or four minutes to get ready to go inside and start arguing. He would look up at the fine house he had bought for his family and wish he was someplace else. Finally he would pick up his briefcase and go on in.

Lelia would be running around the kitchen in a tennis skirt trying to get dinner on the table so Will wouldn't know she hadn't done anything all day but play tennis. Will would say, "Did you call Robert's coach?"

"I couldn't get him on the phone."

"What do you mean, you couldn't get him on the phone? They don't have phones anymore at Horace Green School?"

"Are you accusing me of lying?"

Will McLaurin was not a big man. He was five nine with broad shoulders and curly red hair and black eyes. When he started arguing he lit up like an actor on the stage.

"Lelia, I said did you call the coach or did you not call the coach. Don't make something up. Just answer the question."

Lelia McLaurin looked like a blonde housewife on a television commercial. She had a good figure from playing tennis all the time and she had a bad temper from getting her way all the time.

"I don't have to listen to this. I don't have to hear this while I'm cooking dinner. If you keep this up I'll leave and you can cook your own dinner." She was furiously buttering French bread to go with the fried chicken the cook had left warming in the oven.

"Lelia, listen to me. All I'm asking is did you call Robert's coach or not. I'm not accusing you of anything and I'm not trying to put anything over on you. Did you call Robert's coach and ask him if Robert has been showing up for practice?"

"I left a message but he didn't call back."

"Did you go out and see if he was at practice?"

"I'm not going to spy on my own child. Stop ruining my evening. Have a drink or something. He goes to practice. He bought a new track suit just last week."

"Lelia, will you look at this for a minute. Just look at this and then we won't discuss it anymore," and Will handed her a yellow legal pad with a list printed on the first page.

"What in the hell is this?" She turned toward him fiercely, her pleated skirt twirling around her legs.

"That is a partial list of the furnishings, decorations, and trinkets in our only son's bedroom. I was hoping you might sit down and read it and think about it."

"This legal garbage. This goddamn lawyer list," and Lelia ripped the page from the legal pad and threw it at the pantry door.

The list read:

1. Black light
2. Two strobe lights for altering perception of light
3. Poster of androgynous figure on motorcycle smoking a marijuana cigarette
4. Poster of Peter Fonda smoking a marijuana cigarette
5. Package of sandwich-size baggies, often used to parcel out marijuana into what are known as "lids"
6. 36 long-playing record albums featuring artists who smoke marijuana and advocate the use of various drugs in the lyrics of their songs
7. Recipe, supposedly a joke, for the manufacture of LSD from sunflower seeds

"You have to stop spying on Robert! That's just their way of being cute. He pretends he's in the revolution. I think you hate him."

"If you call walking in his room spying. That is a list of objects that can be seen by a person of normal eyesight standing in the middle of his room."

"You hate him."

"Lelia, I don't hate him. I hate him hanging around the park all the time. I hate him barely passing at school and never reading a book anymore. Lelia, a madness is stalking this city and I don't want to lose my son to it."

They were out in the hall. Lelia was getting a raincoat out

of a closet. It wasn't raining. She was getting out the raincoat because it is hard to walk out on someone wearing only a tennis skirt and a LaCoste shirt. She was crying.

Will took the raincoat away from her and tried to put his arms around her. They hadn't made love to each other for two weeks.

"Look, tomorrow is Friday. Leave Robert with your mother and we'll drive to Biloxi for the weekend. We can lie around in the sun and talk things over. Let's get out of town and try to love each other and see if we can think straight."

"All right. If you won't talk about it anymore tonight. The other day I saw him riding a little black boy around on his handlebars. You've got me so paranoid I thought there was something wrong with that."

"What time tomorrow could you leave?"

"I'm going to the beauty parlor at four. I'll pick you up at the office at five-thirty and we'll take the expressway from downtown. We can stop in Mandeville and have dinner at Begue's."

"Sure we can. Bring a shaker of martinis. We'll drink all the way to the coast like the old days."

Then the McLaurins had a peaceful meal for a change and Will and Lelia went up early to bed.

As soon as they disappeared Robert called up Gus and told him the good news that they would have the house to themselves for the weekend. He smoked a joint and drifted off to sleep listening to his radio. "*Drove my Chevy to the levee but the levee was dry, drove my Chevy to the levee but the levee was dry.*"

Gus was waiting for Robert in the front yard when Robert came home the next day. Gus was excited. He loved the McLaurins' beautiful old house. He had spent the night there once before when Robert had a baby-sitter. Robert had sneaked him in. What Gus really liked was Robert's father's shower. It had an attachment that gave you a massage while you took a shower. Gus said it felt like little pieces of diamonds hitting your skin.

On this particular Friday Robert felt good to be walking in the front door with his friend. The McLaurin house was built around a wide central hall. At the far end of the hall a stair-case five feet wide rose to the second floor. The hall was hung with an amazing assortment of paintings.

"Your momma sure does have a lot of pictures."

"She painted this one herself."

"What's it a picture of?" Gus asked.

"What does it look like to you?"

"A fire. A big field of fire."

"Well, she says it's a picture of the inside of her head when she was going to have me as a baby."

"I wouldn't have guessed it."

The boys went on in the kitchen. They decided to really have a party.

Lelia entered the Magic Slipper Beauty Salon with a sigh. She was exhausted from rushing to get there on time.

"Tim, I'm sorry I'm late. I got in school traffic on the Avenue."

"It's okay, sweetie, but we'll have to skip the manicure. I've got a date at six." He handed her a leopard-printed smock and nodded toward the dressing room. His silver hair was cut in a Prince Valiant. He was vain of his body and his clientele. He put up with a lot from Lelia because she had been named to the list of Beautiful Activists two years in a row before she had turned herself into a tennis-playing machine.

"He's driving me crazy," she said, settling into the sham-poo chair. "Between the two of them I don't care if I live or die. I can't even play tennis worth a damn. I lost every important match I played last week. I'm down to six on the ladder."

"Sweetie, you can't let them do that to you. What does Arthur say?" They shared a psychiatrist. This creates a strange bond between people.

"He says I have to work through it. Will and I are going to the coast for the weekend to talk it over. We may end up sending Robert off to school. Will wants me to treat Robert the way his mother treated him, the old guilt routine. Look what it did to him. He doesn't even know he's neurotic. At least I know I'm neurotic."

"Lelia, is that you?" Danny Adler's mother came up with her hair wrapped in a turban on the way to the back for a pedicure.

"Janet, how are you?"

"Listen, thanks for asking Danny to spend the night. It really worked out beautifully because we are planning on being out late tonight."

"Janet," Lelia sat up, half-rinsed, "Janet, I didn't ask Danny to spend the night. Will and I are going out of town for the weekend. Robert is staying with Mother. Are you sure he said Robert asked him?"

"Yes, he said you-all were taking them to the movies."

Tim started laughing. "The old mom's-out-of-town game. I'll bet they're shacked up with some charmers in your bedroom right this minute."

"I'm going home," Lelia said, "Tim, get this stuff off my hair and comb me out."

"You can't go home like this."

"I don't care. Just comb out my hair. I mean it, Tim. Janet, I'll call you later."

"Sweetie, take a Valium. You want a Valium?"

"Oh, could you, thanks."

Tim fished a bottle out of his pocket. "One or two?"

"Two."

Lelia parked the car two houses away and walked across the lawn and onto her front porch. She felt like a member of the CIA. She could hear the music playing as she walked across the yard. She could hear the music before she stepped onto the porch. She could hear the music and through the floor-length windows of the living room she could see Robert draped over the beige-and-white-striped loveseat holding a cigarette in one hand and nodding dreamily with his eyes closed. She could see the mirrored cocktail table with the silver champagne bucket and the two-hundred-year-old red crystal Madeira glasses beside it. Robert got up and walked into the next room to change the record.

Lelia stepped into the hall.

Gus came walking down the stairs. He came walking down the carpeted stairs and down the wide walnut hall with its sixteen-foot ceilings. He came walking down the hall wrapped in a plush baby-blue monogrammed towel from the Lylian Shop. Pearls of water were dripping down his face from his thick soft hair. Widely grinning, hugely smiling, Gus came down the hall, down the Aubusson runner, down Lelia's schizophrenic, eclectic art gallery of a hall, past the Walter Andersons, the deCallatays, the Leroy Morais, the Rolland Golden, the Stanford, past the portrait of Robert's grandfather in the robes of a state supreme court justice, past the Dufy. He had just passed the edge of the new Leonor Fini when Lelia stepped into the hall and they spotted each other.

Here Gus came, in the baby-blue towel, black as a walnut tree in winter, draped as a tiny emperor, carrying his empty champagne glass in one hand and using the other for an imperial robe clasp. Expansively, ecstatically pleased to be, delighted to be, charmed to be alive on this, the fourteenth day of April, nineteen hundred and seventy-one; he, Gus, man of parts, friend of white man and black man, friend of oak tree, levee, and river, citizen of New Orleans, Louisiana, dope pusher to the Audubon Park, dispenser of the new Nirvana. He, Gus, five feet one inches, one hundred and two pounds of pure D Gus, walking down the hall.

Lelia screamed. She screamed six months of unscreamed screaming. She screamed an ancestral, a territorial scream. She screamed her head off.

"What in the name of God are you doing in my house?" she screamed.

"Robert," she screamed, "what is this black child doing in my house? What is this goddamn black pusher doing in my house? Robert," she screamed, "get in here this second."

Gus's eyes met hers at a forty-degree angle. His huge black eyes met her wide aluminum ones down the long hall and held for a moment and then Gus cut and ran back up the stairs to the bedroom, trailing the towel behind him, his tiny black butt shining in the reflected light from the stained-glass window in the stairway alcove.

Robert ran past his mother's screaming and up the stairs behind Gus and the two boys ran into the master bedroom and slammed the door and threw the safety bolt and Robert stood with his back to the door breathing like a runaway mule.

"What are we gonna do now?" Robert said, his heart pushing against his fake soccer shirt.

"I'm getting out of here. That's what I'm doing," Gus said, pulling on his plaid pants and searching for his boots.

"You can't get out of here. There isn't any way out."

"There's that window," Gus said. "There's that window and that's the way I'm going out." He pointed to a double French window that opened onto a false balcony and overlooked the side yard. The top twelve feet of an old crepe myrtle tree pushed against the balcony waving its clusters of soft pink flowers in the breeze.

"You can't get out there. It's forty feet to the ground."

"I'm going down that tree."

"That's a crepe myrtle. You can't climb down a crepe myrtle."

"If it's the only tree I got, I can climb down it," Gus said, putting on his jacket and pushing open the French doors.

Lelia was beating on the door with her fists.

"Robert, if you don't open this door you will never leave this house again. If you don't open this door this minute you will be sent to Saint Stanislaus. I'll call the police. I've already called your father. He'll be here any minute. You might as well open the door. You better hurry and open this door. You better answer me this minute."

"That's the maddest woman I ever heard in my life," Gus said, throwing one leg over the balcony.

"Don't do it, Gus. Gus, don't do it," Robert said, grabbing him. "She won't really call the police. She's just saying that. It will be all right when my father gets here."

"Let go of me, Robert," Gus warned.

"Robert," she screamed, "if you don't open this door you will be the sorriest boy in New Orleans."

Robert turned to look at the door. He looked past the beautiful white-lacquered four-poster bed with Lelia's favorite sun hats hanging gaily from the bedposts.

As he turned to look at the door Gus shook his head and reached down and bit the freckled hand that held him. He bit Robert's hand as hard as he could bite it and Robert let go.

Gus jumped into the heart of the crepe myrtle tree. He dove into the tree and swayed in its branches like a cat. He steadied, grabbed for a larger branch, found a temporary footing, grabbed again, and began to fall through the up-thrust branches like a bird shot in flight. As Robert watched, Gus came to rest upon the ground, his wet black hair festooned with the soft pink blossoms of the crepe myrtle.

Then, as Robert watched, Gus pushed off from the earth. He began to ascend back up through the broken branches like a movie played in reverse, like a wild kite rising to meet the sun, and Robert was amazed and enchanted by the beauty of this feat and jumped from the window high into the air to join Gus on his journey.

And far away in the loud hall Lelia beat on the door and beat on the door and beat on the door.

There's a Garden of Eden

Scores of men, including an ex-governor and the owner of a football team, consider Alisha Terrebone to be the most beautiful woman in the state of Louisiana. If she is unhappy what hope is there for ordinary mortals? Yet here is Alisha, cold and bored and lonely, smoking in bed.

Not an ordinary bed either. This bed is eight feet wide and covered with a spread made from Alisha's old fur coats. There are dozens of little pillows piled against the headboard, and the sheets are the color of shells and wild plums and ivory.

Everything else in the room is brown, brown velvet, brown satin, brown leather, brown silk, deep polished woods.

Alisha sleeps alone in the wonderful bed. She has a husband, but he isn't any fun anymore. He went morose on Alisha. Now he has a bed of his own in another part of town.

Alisha has had three husbands. First she married a poor engineer and that didn't work out. Then she married a judge and that didn't work out. Then she married a rich lawyer and that didn't work out.

Now she stays in bed most of the day, reading and drinking coffee, listening to music, cutting pictures out of old magazines, dreaming, arguing with herself.

This morning it is raining, the third straight day of the steady dramatic rains that come in the spring to New Orleans.

"It's on the T.V. a flood is coming," the maid says, bringing in Alisha's breakfast tray. Alisha and the maid adore each other. No matter how many husbands Alisha has she always keeps the same old maid.

"They always say a flood is coming," Alisha says. "It gives them something to talk about on television all day."

"I hope you're right," the maid says. "Anyway, your mother's been calling and calling. And the carpenter's here. He wants to start on the kitchen cabinets."

"Oh," Alisha says, "which carpenter?"

"The new one," the maid says, looking down at her shoes. "The young one." Blue-collar workers, she says to herself. Now it's going to be blue-collar workers.

"All right," Alisha says. "Tell him I'll talk to him as soon as I get dressed. Fix him some coffee."

Alisha gets out of bed, runs a comb through her hair, pulls on a pair of brown velvet pants, and ties a loose white shirt around her waist. I've got to get a haircut, she says, tying back her thick black curls with a pink ribbon. I've really got to do something about this hair.

The carpenter's name is Michael. He used to be a Presbyterian. Now he is a Zen Buddhist carpenter. When he uses wood he remembers the tree. Every day he says to himself. *I am part of the universe. I have a right to be here.*

This is something he learned when he was younger, when he was tripping with his wild friends. Michael is through with tripping now. He wants to go straight and have a car that runs. He wants his parents to call him up and write him letters and lend him money. His parents are busy pediatricians. They kicked him out for tripping. They don't have time for silly shit about the universe.

Alisha found Michael in a classified ad. "Household repairs done by an honest, dedicated craftsman. Call after four."

Alisha called the number and he came right over. As soon as she opened the door she knew something funny was going on. What kind of a carpenter shows up in a handmade white peasant shirt carrying a recorder.

"Can I put this somewhere while you show me what needs fixing," he said, looking at her out of dark blue eyes.

"What is it?" she said, taking it from him, laying it on a sofa.

"It's a musical instrument," he said. "I play with a group on Thursday nights. I was on my way there."

39

She led him around the house showing him things that were broken, watching his hands as he touched her possessions, watching his shoulders and his long legs and his soft hair and his dark blue eyes.

"This is a nice house," he said, when he had finished his inspection. "It has nice vibrations. I feel good here."

"It's very quiet," she said.

"I know," he said. "It's like a cave."

"You're right," she said. "It is like a cave. I never would have thought of that."

"Do you live here alone?" he said, holding his recorder in his arms. The last rays of the afternoon sun were filtering in through the leaded glass doors in the hallway casting rainbows all over the side of his face. Alisha was watching the blue part of the rainbow slide along the hollows of his cheeks.

"Most of the time," she said. "I have a husband, but he's almost never here anymore."

"It feels like only one person lives here," he said. "Everything seems to belong to you."

"It's very astute of you to see that," she began in a serious voice, then broke into a giggle. "To tell the truth, that's why my husband left. He said only Kierkegaard would believe I loved him. He said the longer he stayed in this house the smaller he became. He said he had gotten to be about the size of an old golf ball in the corner."

"Why did he let you do that to him?" Michael said.

"He did it to himself," she said. "I don't take responsibility for other people's lives. I don't believe in being a scapegoat. That's a thing Jews are historically pretty good at, you know, so I'm always watching out for it in myself. Women are pretty good at it too, for that matter."

"You're a pretty smart lady."

"No, I'm not," she said. "I'm just trying to make it through the days like everybody else."

"I should be leaving," he said. "I'm having a hard time leaving this house."

"Come back, then," she said. "As soon as you have time. I'm looking forward to getting things fixed up around the place."

Now he was back, leaning on a counter in her spotless

kitchen, cradling a cup of coffee, listening intently to something the maid was telling him.

"Have you been sick?" Michael asked, looking up from his coffee.

"Not really," she said. "I just stay in bed a lot."

"Do you want me to start on these cabinets?" he said. "I could come back another day."

"Oh, no," she said. "Today is fine. It was nice of you to come out in this weather."

"It says on the television two pumping stations are out," the maid said. "It says it's going to flood and your mother's been calling and calling."

"Maybe you should go home then," Alisha said. "Just in case."

"I think I will," the maid said. "They might let the schools out early and I'm taking care of my grandchild this week."

"Go on then," Alisha said. "I can manage here."

"What about the cabinets?" the maid said. "I was going to put in shelf paper when he finished."

"It doesn't matter," Alisha said. "I'll do it. Look out there. The sky is black as it can be. You better call a cab."

Michael finished his coffee, rinsed out the cup in the sink, set it neatly upside down to dry and began to work on the hardware of the cabinet doors, aligning them so they stayed closed when they were shut.

"They go out of tune," he said, "like a piano. I wonder who installed these to begin with. He must have been an impatient man. See how he drove these screws in. I should take the hardware off and start all over."

"Will that take a long time?" she said.

"Well," he laughed, "you'd probably have to refinish the cabinets if I did that."

"Then do it," she said. "Go on. Fix them right while you're here."

"I'll see," he said. "Perhaps I will change the worst ones, like the ones over the stove."

He went back to work. Outside torrents of rain beat against the windows and the sky was black as evening. Alisha moved around the kitchen straightening things inside the cabinets. She had not looked inside these cabinets in ages. She had forgotten all the interesting and beautiful things she owned. There were shelves of fine Limoges china and silver serving pieces wrapped carelessly in cellophane bags from the dry cleaners. There were copper pans and casserole dishes. There were stainless-steel mixing bowls and porcelain soufflé dishes and shelves and shelves of every sort of wineglass from the time when she gave dinner parties. There was one cabinet full of cookbooks and recipe folders and flower vases and candles and candleholders.

She took down a cookbook called *The Joy of Cooking*. Her first mother-in-law had given it to her. On the flyleaf was an inscription, "Much love for good cooking and a few fancy dishes." Underneath the inscription the maid had written TAKE FROM THE LEFT, SERVE FROM THE RIGHT, in large letters.

Alisha laughed out loud.

"What's so funny," the carpenter said.

"I found a book I used to use when I gave dinner parties," she said. "I wasn't very good at dinner parties. I was too ambitious. I used to make things with *curry*. And the maid and I used to get drunk while we were waiting for the guests to arrive. We never could remember which side to serve the vegetables from. No matter how many dinner parties we had we never could remember."

"Why did you get drunk?" Michael said. "Were you unhappy?"

"No," she said. "I don't think so. To tell the truth I think I was hungry. I used to take diet pills so I wouldn't eat any of the good things I was always cooking. I would be so hungry by nighttime I would get drunk if I only had a glass of wine."

"Why did you do all that?" he said, wondering if she always said anything that came into her head.

"I did it so I would look like Audrey Hepburn," she said. "At that time most of the women in the United States wanted to look like Audrey Hepburn."

"Really?" he said.

"Well, all of my friends did at least. I spent most of my waking hours trying not to eat anything. It was a lot of trouble, being hungry all the time."

"It sounds terrible," Michael said. "Do you still do it?"

"No," she said. "I quit giving a damn about Audrey Hepburn. Then I quit taking diet pills, and then I quit drinking, and then I quit giving dinner parties. Then I quit doing anything I didn't like to do."

"What do you like to do?" he asked.

"I don't know," she said. "I haven't found out yet."

"Your phone is ringing," he said. "Aren't you going to answer it?"

"No," she said. "I don't like to talk on the telephone."

"The maid said your mother had been trying to call you."

"I know. That's probably her on the phone now."

"You aren't going to answer it?"

"No. Because I already know what she's going to say. She's going to tell me a flood is coming. Don't pay any attention to the phone. It'll stop in a minute."

He put down his tools and turned around to face her. "There's a whole lot going on in this room right now," he said. "Are you aware of that?" He looked very serious, wiping his hands across his sleeves.

"How old are you?" Alisha said.

"What difference does that make?" he said and crossed the room and put his arms around her. She felt very nice in his arms, soft and brave and sad, like an old actress.

"Oh, my," she said. "I was afraid this was going to happen." Then they laid down their weapons and walked awkwardly down the hall to the bedroom, walking slowly as though they were going to do something embarrassing and awkward and absurd.

At the door to the bedroom he picked her up and carried her to the bed, hoping that was the romantic thing to do. Then he saw it. "What in the name of God is this?" he said, meaning the fur bedspread.

"Something my mother gave me," she said. "Isn't it the tackiest thing you've ever seen in your life."

"Your body is very beautiful," she said when he had taken off his clothes and was standing before her, shy and human. "You *look* like a grown man. That's a relief."

"Do you always say whatever comes into your head?" he said.

"Oh, yes," she said. "I think everyone knows what

everyone else is thinking all the time anyway. Do you mind? Do you think I talk too much?"

"Oh, no," he said. "I like it. It keeps surprising me."

"Do you like my body," she said, for now she had taken off her clothes and had struck a pose, sitting cross-legged on the bed.

"Of course I do," he said. "I've been wanting to touch your tits ever since the first moment I saw you. The whole time we were walking around your house I was wanting to touch your tits."

"Oh, my," she said. "Not my tits again. For years I believed men liked me for my mind. Imagine that! I read hundreds of books so they would like me better. All the time they were only wanting to touch my tits. Think of that!"

"Now you're talking too much," he said.

Then Alisha closed her eyes and pretended she was an Indian princess lying in a tent deep in a forest, dressed in a long white deerskin robe, waiting for Jeff Chandler to come and claim her for his bride. Outside the wind and rain beat down upon the forest.

Then Michael closed his eyes and pretended he was a millionaire going to bed with a beautiful, sad old actress.

The phone woke them with its ringing. Alisha was startled for a moment. Then she settled back down, remembering where she was. Michael's legs were smooth and warm beside her. She was safe.

"You really ought to answer that," he said. "This is quite a storm we're having."

She picked his shirt up off the floor, put it on for a bathrobe, and went into the other room to talk.

"That was my mother," she reported. "She's crying. She's almost got her companion crying. I think they're both crying. He's this real sensitive young man we found in the drama department at Tulane. They watch T.V. together. He's learning to be an actor watching T.V."

"Why is she crying?" Michael said, sitting up in bed, pulling the plum-colored sheets around his waist.

"She's crying because the basement of her house is flooding. It always does that in heavy rains. She lives on Jefferson

Avenue, around the corner. Anyway, she can't find one of her cats and she thinks he's getting wet."

"Her cats?"

"She has six or seven cats. At least six cats. Anyway, she thinks the water is going to keep on rising and drown her cats."

"You'd better go and see about her then. We'd better go and help her."

"Help her? How can we help her? It's a flash flood on Jefferson Avenue. It'll go away as soon as the pumping stations start working. I told her to sell that goddamn house the last time this happened."

"It's flooding your mother's house and you don't want to go and help her?"

"It's only flooding the basement."

"How old is she?"

"My mother. She's seventy-eight. She has a companion. Besides, she does anything she wants to do. Last year she went to *China*. She's perfectly all right."

"Then why is she crying?"

"Because she thinks her silly goddamn cats are getting wet."

"Then we'll have to go and help her."

"How can we. It's *flooded* all the way down Jefferson Avenue."

"Does that canoe in the garage work?"

"I think so. No one's ever used it. Stanley ordered it last year when he got interested in the Sierra Club. But no one's ever *used* it."

"Then we'll go in that. Every time I see a flood on television and people going to get other people in boats I want to be one of them. This is my chance. We can take the canoe in my truck to where the water starts. Go on. Call your mother back and tell her we're coming to save her. Tell her we'll be right there. And, Alisha."

"Yes."

"Tell her to stop crying. After all, she is your mother."

"This is a great canoe," he said, maneuvering it down from the floored platform of the garage. "Your husband never uses it?"

45

"He never uses anything," she said. "He just likes to have things. To tell the truth he's almost never here."

"Then why are you married?" he asked.

"That's a good question," Alisha said. "But I don't know the answer to it."

"Well, look, let's go on over there. I can't wait to put this in the water. I'm afraid the water will go down before we get there."

"It's really nice of you to do this," Alisha said, standing close to him, smelling the warm smell of his clothes, taking everything that she could get while she could get it.

"Everybody loves to be a hero," Michael said, putting his arms around her again, running his hands up and down her strange soft body.

"Say I'm not your mother," she said.

"You're not my mother," he said. "Besides, it doesn't matter. We're probably only dreaming."

They drove down Freret Street with the city spread out before them, clean and shining after the rain. The sun was lighting up the red tile roofs of the houses, and Tulane students were on the porches with glasses in their hands, starting their flood parties.

The inside of Michael's truck was very cosy. He used it for a business office. File folders stuffed with bills and invoices were piled in one corner, and an accounting book was on the dashboard.

"Will I make love to you again?" Alisha said, for she was too old to play hard to get.

"Whenever you want to," he said. "As soon as we finish saving your mother."

They could see the flood now. They took the canoe out of the back of the truck and carried it to where the water began at the foot of Skippy Nevelson's front yard. Alisha sat in the bow and Michael waded out pushing her until it was deep enough for him to climb in.

"I don't believe I'm doing this," she said. "You're the craziest man I ever met in my life."

"Which way is the house," he said.

"It's the second house off Willow," Alisha said. "I guess we'll just go down Jefferson and take a right at Willow."

They floated along with Michael paddling. The water was three feet deep, thick and brown and slow-moving. An envelope floated by, then an orange barrette, then a purple Frisbee.

Alisha was feeling wonderful. If Skippy Nevelson was leaning out of her front window with her eyes the size of plates, if the WDSU Minicam crew was filming her for the evening news, if the levee broke and carried them all out to sea, what was that to Alisha, who had been delivered of an angel.

"What will happen next?" she asked, pushing her luck.

"Whatever we want to happen," he said, lifting the paddle and throwing the muddy water up into the air.

"Oh, my," she said to no one in particular. "This was the year I was going to stop dying my hair."

Now they were only a block away from their destination. Alisha kept her face to the front wishing she had a hat so Michael couldn't see her wrinkles. I have to remember this a long time, she told herself. I have to watch everything and hear everything and smell everything and remember everything. This may have to last me a long, long time.

Then Alisha did a stupid thing. She wrote a little script for herself. This is the very last time I will ever love anyone she told herself. I will love this boy until he leaves me. And then I will never love another human being.

And he will leave me, because no man has ever left me in my whole life and sooner or later it has to be my turn. After a while he will stop loving me and nothing will bring him back, not all the money or love or passion in the world will hold him. So he will leave me and go into the future and I will stay here and remember love. *And that is what I get for devoting my life to love instead of wisdom.*

So Alisha sat in the bow and wrote a script for herself and then she went to work to make it all come true.

"There it is," she said, spotting the house. "The one with the green awnings. See the balconies on the top. When I was a child I always dreamed of walking out there and waving to people, but the windows were always locked so I wouldn't fall to my death on Willow Street."

"That's terrible," he said. "You had a fancy place like that and you couldn't even walk out on the balconies."

"I couldn't do anything," she said. "They were too afraid I'd get hurt. That's how wealthy Jews used to raise their children. They didn't let me ride a bicycle or roller skate or swim or anything."

"You don't know how to *swim!*" he said.

"No," she said. "Isn't that dreadful?"

"Then what are you doing in this boat?"

"Hoping it won't turn over," she said, smiling a wonderful mysterious French smile, holding on lightly to the gunwales while he rowed her to her mother's doorstep.

The Famous Poll at Jody's Bar

It was ninety-eight degrees in the shade in New Orleans, a record-breaking day in August.

Nora Jane Whittington sat in a small apartment several blocks from Jody's Bar and went over her alternatives.

"No two ways about it," she said to herself, shaking out her black curls, "if Sandy wants my ass in San Jose, I'm taking it to San Jose. But I've got to get some cash."

Nora Jane was nineteen years old, a self-taught anarchist and a quick-change artist. She owned six Dynel wigs in different hair colors, a makeup kit she stole from Le Petit Theatre du Vieux Carre while working as a volunteer stagehand, and a small but versatile wardrobe. She could turn her graceful body into any character she saw in a movie or on T.V. Her specialties were boyish young lesbians, boyish young nuns, and a variety of lady tourists.

Nora Jane could also do wonderful tricks with her voice, which had a range of almost two octaves. She was the despair of the sisters at the Academy of the Most Holy Name of Jesus when she quit the choir saying her chores at home didn't allow her to stay after school to practice.

The sisters made special novenas for the bright, lonely child whose father died at the beginning of the Vietnam War and whose pretty alcoholic mother wept and prayed when they called upon her begging her to either put away the bottle and make a decent home for Nora Jane or allow them to put her in a Catholic boarding school.

Nora Jane didn't want a decent home. What she wanted was a steady boyfriend, and the summer she graduated from high school she met Sandy. Nora Jane had a job selling records at The Mushroom Cloud, a record shop near the Tulane campus where rich kids came to spend their parents' money on phonograph records and jewelry made in the shape of coke spoons and marijuana leaves. "The Cloud" was a nice place, up a flight of narrow stairs from Freret Street. Nora Jane felt important, helping customers decide what records to buy.

The day Sandy came into her life she was wearing a yellow cotton dress and her hair was curling around her face from the humidity.

Sandy walked into the shop and stood for a long time reading the backs of jazz albums. He was fresh out of a Texas reform school with $500.00 in the bank and a new lease on life. He was a handsome boy with green eyes as opaque and unfathomable as a salt lake. When he smiled down at Nora Jane over a picture of Rahshaan Roland Kirk as The Five Thousand Pound Man, she dreamed of Robert Redford as The Sundance Kid.

"I'm going to dedicate a book of poems to this man's memory," Sandy said. "I'm going to call the book *Dark Mondays*. Did you know that Rahshaan Kirk died last year?"

"I don't know much about him. I haven't been working here long," Nora Jane said. "Are you really a writer?"

"I'm really a land surveyor, but I write poems and stories at night. In the school I went to in Texas a poet used to come and teach my English class once a month. He said the most important writing gets done in your head while you think you're doing something else. Sometimes I write in the fields while I'm working. I sing the poems I'm writing to myself like work songs. Then at night I write them down. You really ought to listen to this album. Rahshaan Kirk is almost as good as Coltrane. A boy I went to school with is his cousin."

"I guess I have a lot to learn about different kinds of music," Nora Jane answered, embarrassed.

"I'm new in town," Sandy said, after they had talked for a while, "and I don't know many people here yet. How about going with me to a political rally this afternoon. I read in the paper that The Alliance for Good Government is having a free picnic in Audubon Park. I like to find out what's going on in politics when I get to a new town."

"I don't know if I should," Nora Jane said, trying not to smile.

"It's all right," Sandy told her. "I'm really a nice guy. You'll be safe with me. It isn't far from here and we have to walk anyway because I don't have a car, so if you don't like it you can just walk away. If you'll go I'll wait for you after work."

"I guess I should go," Nora Jane said. "I need to know what's going on in politics myself."

When Nora Jane was through for the day they walked to Audubon Park and ate free fried chicken and listened to the Democratic candidate for the House of Representatives debate the Republican candidate over the ERA and the canal treaties.

It was still light when they walked back through the park in the direction of Sandy's apartment. Nora Jane was telling Sandy the story of her life. She had just gotten to the sad part where her father died when he stopped her and put his hands around her waist.

"Wait just a minute," he said, and he walked over to the roots of an enormous old live-oak tree and began to dig a hole with the heel of his boot. When he had dug down about six inches in the hard-packed brown soil he took out all the change he had in his pockets, wrapped it in a dollar bill and buried it in the hole. He packed the dirt back down with his hands and looked up at her.

"Remember this spot," he said, "you might need this some day."

Many hours later Nora Jane reached out and touched his arm where he stood leaning into the window frame watching the moon in the cloudy sky.

"Do you want to stay here for a while?" he asked, without looking at her.

"I want to stay here for a long time," she answered, taking a chance.

So she stayed for fourteen months.

Sandy taught her how to listen to jazz, how to bring a kite down without tearing it, how to watch the sun go down on the Mississippi River, how to make macrame plant holders out of kite string, and how to steal things.

Stealing small things from elegant uptown gift shops was as easy as walking down a tree-lined street. After all, Sandy assured her, their insurance was covering it. Pulling off robberies was another thing. Nora Jane drove the borrowed getaway car three times while Sandy cleaned out a drugstore and two beauty parlors in remote parts of Jefferson Parish. The last of these jobs supplied her with the wigs. Sandy picked them up for her on his way out.

"I'm heading for the west coast," he told her, when the beauty parlor job turned out to be successful beyond his wildest dreams, netting them $723.00. He had lucked into a payroll.

"I'll send for you as soon as I get settled," he said, and he lifted her over his head like a flower and carried her to the small iron bed and made love to her while the afternoon sun and then the moonlight poured in the low windows of the attic apartment.

Robbing a neighborhood bar in uptown New Orleans in broad daylight all by herself was another thing entirely. Nora Jane thought that up for herself. It was the plan she settled upon as the quickest way to get to California. She planned it for weeks, casing the bar at different times of the day and night in several disguises, and even dropping by one Saturday afternoon pretending to be collecting money to help the Crippled Children's Hospital. She collected almost ten dollars.

Nora Jane had never been out of the state of Louisiana, but once she settled on a plan of action she was certain all she needed was a little luck and she was as good as wading in the Pacific Ocean. One evening's work and her hands were back in Sandy's hair.

She crossed herself and prayed for divine intervention. After all, she told herself, robbing an old guy who sold whiskey and laid bets on athletic events was part of an anarchist's work. Nora Jane didn't like old guys much anyway. They were all wrinkled where the muscles ought to be and they were so sad.

She took the heavy stage pistol out of its hiding place under the sink and inspected it. She practiced looking tough for a few minutes and then replaced the gun in its wrapper and sat down at the card table to go over her plans.

Nora Jane had a methodical streak and liked to take care of details.

"The first nigger that comes in here attempting a robbery is going to be in the wrong place," Jody laughed, smiling at Judge Crozier and handing him a fresh bourbon and Coke across the bar.

"Yes, sir, that nigger is gonna be in the wrong place." Jody fingered the blackjack that lay in its purple velvet sack on a small shelf below the antiquated cash register and warmed into his favorite subject, his interest in local crime fueled by a report in the *Times-Picayune* of a holdup in a neighborhood Tote-Sum store.

The black bandits had made the customers lie on the floor, cleaned out the cash register, and helped themselves to a cherry Icee on the way out. The newspaper carried a photograph of the Icee machine.

The judge popped open his third sack of Bar-B-Que potato chips and looked thoughtful. The other customers waited politely to see what he had to say for himself this morning concerning law and order.

"Now, Jody, you don't know how a man will act in an emergency until that emergency transpires," the judge began, wiping his hands on his worn seersucker pants. "That's a fact and worthy of all good men to be accepted. Your wife could be in here helping tend bar. Your tables could be full of innocent customers watching a ball game. You might be busy talking to someone like that sweet little girl who came in last Saturday collecting for the Crippled Children's Hospital. First thing you know, gun in your back, knife at your throat. It has nothing at all to do with being brave." The judge polished off his drink and turned to look out the door to where the poll was going on.

Jody's Bar didn't cater to just anyone that happened to drop by to get a drink or lay a bet. It was the oldest neighborhood bar in the Irish Channel section of New Orleans, and its regular customers included second- and third-generation drinkers from many walks of life. Descendants of Creole blue bloods mingled easily with house painters and deliverymen stopping by for a quick one on their route.

Jody ran a notoriously tight ship. No one but Jody himself

had ever answered the telephone that sat beneath a framed copy of The Auburn Creed, and no woman, no matter what her tale of woe, had ever managed to get him to call a man to the phone.

"Not here," he would answer curtly, "haven't seen him." And Jody would hang up without offering to take a message. If a woman wanted a man at Jody's she had to come look for him in person.

There was an air of anticipation around Jody's this Saturday morning. All eight of the stools were filled. The excitement was due to the poll.

Outside of Jody's, seated at a small card table underneath a green-and-white-striped awning, Wesley Labouisse was proceeding with the poll in a businesslike manner. Every male passerby was interviewed in turn and his ballot folded into quarters and deposited in the Mason jar with a pink ribbon from an old Valentine's box wrapped loosely around it.

"Just mark it yes or no. Whatever advice you would give your closest friend if he came to you and told you he was thinking of getting married." Wesley was talking to a fourteen-year-old boy straddling a ten-speed bike.

"Take all the time you need to make up your mind. Think about your mother and father. Think about what it's like to have a woman tell you when to come home every night and when to get up in the morning and when to take a bath and when to talk and when to shut up. Think about what it's like to give your money to a woman from now till the day you die. Then just write down your honest feelings about whether a perfectly happy man ought to go out and get himself married."

Wesley was in a good mood. He had thought up the poll himself and had side bets laid all the way from The New Orleans Country Club to the Plaquemines Parish sheriff's office.

There was a big sign tacked up over the card table declaring THIS POLL IS BEING CONDUCTED WITHOUT REGARD TO SEX OR PREVIOUS CONDITION OF SERVITUDE. Wesley had made the sign himself and thought it was hilarious. He was well known in New Orleans society as the author of Boston Club Mardi Gras skits.

The leading man in the drama of the poll, Prescott Hamilton IV, was leaning into Jody's pinball machine with the dedication of a ballet dancer winding up *The Firebird*. He was twelve games ahead and his brand-new, navy blue wedding suit hung in its plastic see-through wrapper on the edge of the machine swaying in rhythm as Prescott nudged the laws of pinball machines gently in his favor. He was a lucky gambler and an ace pinball-machine player. He was a general favorite at Jody's, where the less aristocratic customers loved him for his gentle ways and his notoriously hollow leg.

Prescott wasn't pretending to be more interested in the outcome of the pinball-machine game than in the outcome of the poll that was deciding his matrimonial future. He was genuinely more interested in the pinball machine. Prescott had great powers of concentration and was a man who lived in the present.

Prescott didn't really care whether he married Emily Anne Hughes or not. He and Emily Anne had been getting alone fine for years without getting married, and he didn't see what difference his moving into Emily Anne's house at this late date was going to make in the history of the world.

Besides he wasn't certain how his Labradors would adjust to her backyard. Emily Anne's house was nice, but the yard was full of little fences and lacked a shade tree.

Nonetheless, Prescott was a man of his word, and if the poll came out in favor of marriage they would be married as soon as he could change into his suit and find an Episcopal minister, unless Emily Anne would be reasonable and settle for the judge.

Prescott was forty-eight years old. The wild blood of his pioneer ancestors had slowed down in Prescott. Even his smile took a long time to develop, feeling out the terrain, then opening up like a child's.

"Crime wave, crime wave, that's all I hear around this place anymore," the judge muttered, tapping his cigar on the edge of the bar and staring straight at the rack of potato chips. "Let's talk about something else for a change."

"Judge, you ought to get Jody to take you back to the

ladies' room and show you the job Claiborne did of patching the window so kids on the street can't see into the ladies'," one of the regulars said. Two or three guys laughed, holding their stomachs.

"Claiborne owed Jody sixty bucks on his tab and the window was broken out in the ladies' room so Jody's old lady talked him into letting Claiborne fix the window to pay back part of the money he owes. After all, Claiborne is supposed to be a carpenter." Everyone started laughing again.

"Well, Claiborne showed up about six sheets in the wind last Wednesday while Jody was out jogging in the park and he went to work. You wouldn't believe what he did. He boarded up the window. He didn't feel like going out for a windowpane, so he just boarded up the window with scrap lumber."

"I'll have to see that as soon as it calms down around here," the judge said, and he turned to watch Prescott who was staring passionately into the lighted TILT sign on the pinball machine.

"What's wrong, Prescott," he said, "you losing your touch?"

"Could be, Judge," Prescott answered, slipping another quarter into the slot.

The late afternoon sun shone in the windows of the bare apartment. Nora Jane had dumped most of her possessions into a container for The Volunteers of America. She had even burned Sandy's letters. If she was caught there was no sense in involving him.

If she was caught what could they do to her, a young girl, a first offender, the daughter of a hero? The sisters would come to her rescue. Nora Jane had carefully been attending early morning mass for several weeks.

She trembled with excitement and glanced at her watch. She shook her head and walked over to the mirror on the dresser. Nora Jane couldn't decide if she was frightened or not. She looked deep into her eyes in the mirror trying to read the secrets of her mind, but Nora Jane was too much in love to even know her own secrets. She was inside a mystery deeper than the mass.

She inspected the reddish-blond wig with its cascades of

silky Dynel falling around her shoulders and blinked her black eyelashes. To the wig and eyelashes she added blue eye shadow, peach rouge and beige lipstick. Nora Jane looked awful.

"You look like a piece of shit," she said to her reflection, adding another layer of lipstick. "Anyway, it's time to go."

On weekends six o'clock was the slow hour at Jody's, when most of the customers went home to change for the evening.

Nora Jane walked down the two flights of stairs and out onto the sidewalk carrying the brown leather bag. Inside was her costume change and a bus ticket to San Francisco zippered into a side compartment. The gun was stuffed into one of the Red Cross shoes she had bought to wear with the short brown nun's habit she had stolen from Dominican College. She hoped the short veil wasn't getting wrinkled. Nora Jane was prissy about her appearance.

As she walked along in the August evening she dreamed of Sandy sitting on her bed playing his harmonica while she pretended to sleep. In the dream he was playing an old Bob Dylan love song, the sort of thing she liked to listen to before he upgraded her taste in music.

Earlier that afternoon Nora Jane had rolled a pair of shorts, an old shirt, and some sandals into a neat bundle and hidden it in the low-hanging branches of the oak tree where Sandy had planted her money.

A scrawny-looking black kid was dozing in the roots of the tree. He promised to keep an eye on her things.

"If I don't come back by tomorrow afternoon you can have this stuff," she told him. "The sandals were handmade in Brazil."

"Thanks," the black kid said. "I'll watch it for you till then. You running away from home or what?"

"I'm going to rob a bank," she confided.

The black kid giggled and shot her the old peace sign.

Wesley walked into the bar where Prescott, Jody, and the judge were all alone watching the evening news on television.

"Aren't you getting tired of that goddamn poll," Prescott said to him. "Emily Anne won't even answer her phone. A joke's a joke, Wesley. I better put on my suit and get on over there."

"Not yet," Wesley said. "The sun isn't all the way down yet. Wait till we open the jar. You promised." Prescott was drunk, but Wesley was drunker. Not that either of them ever showed their whiskey.

"I promised I wouldn't get married unless you found one boy or man all day who thought it was an unqualified good idea to get married. I didn't ever say I was interested in waiting around for the outcome of a vote. Come on and open up that jar before Emily Anne gets any madder."

"What makes you think there is a single ballot in favor of you getting married?" Wesley asked.

"I don't know if there is or there isn't," Prescott answered. "So go on and let the judge open that goddamn jar."

"Look at him, Wesley," Jody said delightedly. "He ain't even signed the papers yet and he's already acting like a married man. Already worried about getting home in time for dinner. If Miss Emily Anne Hughes wakes up in the morning wearing a ring from Prescott, I say she takes the cake. I say she's gone and caught a whale on a ten-pound test line."

"Open the jar," Prescott demanded, while the others howled with laughter.

Nora Jane stepped into the bar, closed the door behind her, and turned the lock. She kept the pistol pointed at the four men who were clustered around the cash register.

"Please be quiet and put your hands over your heads before I kill one of you," she said politely, waving the gun with one hand and reaching behind herself with the other to draw the window shade that said CLOSED in red letters.

Prescott and the judge raised their hands first, then Wesley.

"Do as you are told," the judge said to Jody in his deep voice. "Jody, do what that woman tells you to do and do it this instant." Jody added his hands to the six already pointing at the ceiling fan.

"Get in there," Nora Jane directed, indicating the ladies' room at the end of the bar. "Please hurry before you make me angry. I ran away from DePaul's Hospital yesterday afternoon and I haven't had my medication and I become angry very easily."

The judge held the door open, and the four men crowded into the small bathroom.

"Face the window," Nora Jane ordered, indicating Claiborne's famous repair job. The astonished men obeyed silently as she closed the bathroom door and turned the skeleton key in its lock and dropped it on the floor under the bar.

"Please be very quiet so I won't get worried and need to shoot through the door," she said. "Be awfully quiet. I am an alcoholic and I need some of this whiskey. I need some whiskey in the worst way."

Nora Jane changed into the nun's habit, wiping the makeup off her face with a bar rag and stuffing the old clothes into the bag. Next she opened the cash register, removed all the bills without counting them, and dropped them into the bag. On second thought she added the pile of IOUs and walked back to the door of the ladies' room.

"Please be a little quieter," she said in a husky voice. "I'm getting very nervous."

"Don't worry, Miss. We are cooperating to the fullest extent," the judge's bench voice answered.

"That's nice," Nora Jane said. "That's very nice."

She pinned the little veil to her hair, picked up the bag, and walked out the door. She looked all around, but there was no one on the street but a couple of kids riding tricycles.

As she passed the card table she stopped, marked a ballot, folded it neatly, and dropped it into the Mason jar.

Then, like a woman in a dream, she walked on down the street, the rays of the setting sun making her a path all the way to the bus stop at the corner of Annunciation and Nashville Avenue.

Making her a path all the way to mountains and valleys and fields, to rivers and streams and oceans. To a boy who was like no other. To the source of all water.

In the Land of Dreamy Dreams

On the third of May, 1977, LaGrande McGruder drove out onto the Huey P. Long Bridge, dropped two Davis Classics and a gut-strung PDP tournament racket into the Mississippi River, and quit playing tennis forever.

"That was it," she said. "That was the last goddamn straw." She heaved a sigh, thinking this must be what it feels like to die, to be through with something that was more trouble than it was worth.

As long as she could remember LaGrande had been playing tennis four or five hours a day whenever it wasn't raining or she didn't have a funeral to attend. In her father's law office was a whole cabinet full of her trophies.

After the rackets sank LaGrande dumped a can of brand-new Slazenger tennis balls into the river and stood for a long time watching the cheerful, little, yellow constellation form and re-form in the muddy current.

"Jesus Fucking A Christ," she said to herself. "Oh, well," she added, "maybe now I can get my arms to be the same size for the first time in my life."

LaGrande leaned into the bridge railing, staring past the white circles on her wrists, souvenirs of twenty years of wearing sweatbands in the fierce New Orleans sunlight, and on down to the river where the little yellow constellation was overtaking a barge.

"That goddamn little new-rich Yankee bitch," she said, kicking the bridge with her leather Tretorns.

There was no denying it. There was no undoing it. At ten o'clock that morning LaGrande McGruder, whose grandfather had been president of the United States Lawn Tennis Association, had cheated a crippled girl out of a tennis match, had deliberately and without hesitation made a bad call in the last point of a crucial game, had defended the call against loud protests, taken a big drink of her Gatorade, and proceeded to win the next twelve games while her opponent reeled with disbelief at being done out of her victory.

At exactly three minutes after ten that morning she had looked across the net at the impassive face of the interloper who was about to humiliate her at her own tennis club and she had changed her mind about honor quicker than the speed of light. "Out," she had said, not giving a damn whether the serve was in or out. "Nice try."

"It couldn't be out," the crippled girl said. "Are you sure?"

"Of course I'm sure," LaGrande said. "I wouldn't have called it unless I was sure."

"Are you positive?" the crippled girl said.

"For God's sake," LaGrande said, "look, if you don't mind, let's hurry up and get this over with. I have to be at the country club for lunch." That ought to get her, LaGrande thought. At least they don't let Jews into the country club yet. At least that's still sacred.

"Serving," the crippled girl said, trying to control her rage.

LaGrande took her position at the back of the court, reached up to adjust her visor, and caught the eye of old Claiborne Redding, who was sitting on the second-floor balcony watching the match. He smiled and waved. How long has he been standing there, LaGrande wondered. How long has that old fart been watching me? But she was too busy to worry about Claiborne now. She had a tennis match to save, and she was going to save it if it was the last thing she ever did in her life.

The crippled girl set her mouth into a tight line and prepared to serve into the forehand court. Her name was Roxanne Miller, and she had traveled a long way to this morning's fury. She had spent thousands of dollars on private tennis lessons, hundreds of dollars on equipment, and untold time and energy giving cocktail parties and dinner parties for the entrenched players who one by one she had courted and blackmailed and finagled into giving her matches and return matches until finally one day she would catch them at a weak moment and defeat them. She kept a mental list of such victories. Sometimes when she went to bed at night she would pull the pillows over her head and lie there imagining herself as a sort of Greek figure of justice, sitting on a marble chair in the clouds, holding a scroll, a little parable of conquest and revenge.

It had taken Roxanne five years to fight and claw and worm her way into the ranks of respected Lawn Tennis Club Ladies. For five years she had dragged her bad foot around the carefully manicured courts of the oldest and snottiest tennis club in the United States of America.

For months now her ambitions had centered around La-Grande. A victory over LaGrande would mean she had arrived in the top echelons of the Lawn Tennis Club Ladies.

A victory over LaGrande would surely be followed by invitations to play in the top doubles games, perhaps even in the famous Thursday foursome that played on Rena Clark's private tennis court. Who knows, Roxanne dreamed, La-Grande might even ask her to be her doubles partner. La-Grande's old doubles partners were always retiring to have babies. At any moment she might need a new one. Roxanne would be there waiting, the indefatigable handicapped wonder of the New Orleans tennis world.

She had envisioned this morning's victory a thousand times, had seen herself walking up to the net to shake La-Grande's hand, had planned her little speech of condolence, after which the two of them would go into the snack bar for lunch and have a heart-to-heart talk about rackets and balls and backhands and forehands and volleys and lobs.

Roxanne basked in her dreams. It did not bother her that LaGrande never returned her phone calls, avoided her at the club, made vacant replies to her requests for matches. Roxanne had plenty of time. She could wait. Sooner or later she would catch LaGrande in a weak moment.

That moment came at the club's 100th Anniversary Celebration. Everyone was drunk and full of camaraderie. The old members were all on their best behavior, trying to be extra nice to the new members and pretend like the new members were just as good as they were even if they didn't belong to the Boston Club or the Southern Yacht Club or Comus or Momus or Proteus.

Roxanne cornered LaGrande while she was talking to a famous psychiatrist-player from Washington, a bachelor who was much adored in tennis circles for his wit and political connections.

LaGrande was trying to impress him with how sane she was and hated to let him see her irritation when Roxanne moved in on them.

"When are you going to give me that match you promised me?" Roxanne asked, looking wistful, as if this were something the two of them had been discussing for years.

"I don't know," LaGrande said. "I guess I just stay so busy. This is Semmes Talbot, from Washington. This is Roxanne, Semmes. I'm sorry. I can't remember your last name. You'll have to help me."

"Miller," Roxanne said. "My name is Miller. Really now, when will you play with me?"

"Well, how about Monday?" LaGrande heard herself saying. "I guess I could do it Monday. My doubles game was canceled." She looked up at the doctor to see if he appreciated how charming she was to everyone, no matter who they were.

"Fine," Roxanne said. "Monday's fine. I'll be here at nine. I'll be counting on it so don't let me down." She laughed. "I thought you'd never say yes. I was beginning to think you were afraid I'd beat you."

"Oh, my goodness," LaGrande said, "anyone can beat me, I don't take tennis very seriously anymore, you know. I just play enough to keep my hand in."

"Who was that?" Semmes asked when Roxanne left them. "She certainly has her nerve!"

"She's one of the new members," LaGrande said. "I really try so hard not to be snotty about them. I really do believe that every human being is just as valuable as everyone else, don't you? And it doesn't matter a bit to me what anyone's background is, but some of the new people are sort of hard to take. They're so, oh, well, so *eager*."

Semmes looked down the front of her silk blouse and laughed happily into her aristocratic eyes. "Well, watch out for that one," he said. "There's no reason for anyone as pretty as you to let people make you uncomfortable."

Across the room Roxanne collected Willie and got ready to leave the party. She was on her way home to begin training for the match.

Willie was glad to leave. He didn't like hanging around places where he wasn't wanted. He couldn't imagine why Roxanne wanted to spend all her time playing tennis with a bunch of snotty people.

Roxanne and Willie were new members. Willie's brand-new 15 million dollars and the New Orleans Lawn Tennis Club's brand-new $700,000 dollar mortgage had met at a point in history, and Willie's application for membership had been approved by the board and railroaded past the watchful noses of old Claiborne Redding and his buddies. Until then the only Jewish member of the club had been a globe-trotting Jewish bachelor who knew his wines, entertained lavishly at Antoine's, and had the courtesy to stay in Europe most of the time.

Willie and Roxanne were something else again. "What in the hell are we going to do with a guy who sells ties and a crippled woman who runs around Audubon Park all day in a pair of tennis shorts," Claiborne said, pulling on a pair of the thick white Australian wool socks he wore to play in. The committee had cornered him in the locker room.

"The membership's not for him," they said. "He doesn't even play. You'll never see him. And she really isn't a cripple. One leg is a little bit shorter than the other one, that's all."

"I don't know," Claiborne said. "Not just Jews, for God's sake, but Yankee Jews to boot."

"The company's listed on the American Stock Exchange, Claiborne. It was selling at 16½ this morning, up from 5. And he buys his insurance from me. Come on, you'll never see them All she's going to do is play a little tennis with the ladies."

Old Claiborne rued the day he had let himself be talked into Roxanne and Willie. The club had been forced to take in thirty new families to pay for its new building and some of them were Jews, but, as Claiborne was fond of saying, at least the rest of them tried to act like white people.

Roxanne was something else. It seemed to him that she lived at the club The only person who hung around the club more than Roxanne was old Claiborne himself. Pretty soon she was running the place. She wrote *The Lawn Tennis Newsletter*. She circulated petitions to change the all-white dress rule. She campaigned for more court privileges for women. She dashed in and out of the bar and the dining room making plans with the waiters and chefs for Mixed Doubles Nights, Round Robin Galas, Benefit Children's Jamborees, Saturday Night Luaus.

Claiborne felt like his club was being turned into a cruise ship.

On top of everything else Roxanne was always trying to get in good with Claiborne. Every time he settled down on the balcony to watch a match she came around trying to talk to him, talking while the match was going on, remembering the names of his grandchildren, complimenting him on their serves and backhands and footwork, taking every conceivable liberty, as if at any moment she might start showing up at their weddings and debuts.

Claiborne thought about Roxanne a lot. He was thinking about her this morning when he arrived at the club and saw her cream-colored Rolls-Royce blocking his view of the Garth Humphries Memorial Plaque. He was thinking about her as he got a cup of coffee from a stand the ladies had taken to setting up by the sign-in board. This was some more of her meddling, he thought, percolated coffee in Styrofoam cups with plastic spoons and some kind of powder instead of cream.

At the old clubhouse waiters had brought steaming cups of thick chicory-flavored café au lait out onto the balcony with cream and sugar in silver servers.

Claiborne heaved a sigh, pulled his pants out of his crotch, and went up to the balcony to see what the morning would bring.

He had hardly reached the top of the stairs when he saw Roxanne leading LaGrande to a deserted court at the end of the property. My God in Heaven, he thought, how did she pull that off? How in the name of God did she get hold of Leland's daughter.

Leland McGruder had been Claiborne's doubles partner in their youth. Together they had known victory and defeat in New Orleans and Jackson and Monroe and Shreveport and Mobile and Atlanta and as far away as Forest Hills during one never to be forgotten year when they had thrown their rackets into a red Ford and gone off together on the tour.

Down on the court LaGrande was so aggravated she could barely be civil. How did I end up here, she thought, playing second-class tennis against anyone who corners me at a party.

LaGrande was in a bad mood all around. The psychiatrist had squired her around all weekend, fucked her dispassionately in someone's *garçonnière*, and gone back to Washington without making further plans to see her.

She bounced a ball up and down a few times with her racket, thinking about a line of poetry that kept occurring to her lately whenever she played tennis. "Their only monument the asphalt road, and a thousand lost golf balls."

"Are you coming to Ladies Day on Wednesday?" Roxanne was saying, "we're going to have a great time. You really ought to come. We've got a real clown coming to give out helium balloons, and we're going to photograph the winners sitting on his lap for the newsletter. Isn't that a cute idea?"

"I'm afraid I'm busy Wednesday," LaGrande said, imagining balloons flying all over the courts when the serious players arrived for their noon games. "Look," she said, "let's go on and get started. I can't stay too long."

They set down their pitchers of Gatorade, put on their visors and sweatbands, sprayed a little powdered resin on their hands, and walked out to their respective sides of the court.

Before they hit the ball four times LaGrande knew something was wrong. The woman wasn't going to warm her up! LaGrande had hit her three nice long smooth balls and each time Roxanne moved up to the net and put the ball away on the sidelines.

"How about hitting me some forehands," LaGrande said. "I haven't played in a week. I need to warm up."

"I'll try," Roxanne said, "I have to play most of my game at the net, you know, because of my leg."

"Well, stay back there and hit me some to warm up with," LaGrande said, but Roxanne went right on putting her shots away with an assortment of tricks that looked more like a circus act than a tennis game.

66

"Are you ready to play yet?" she asked. "I'd like to get started before I get too tired."

"Sure," LaGrande said. "Go ahead, you serve first. There's no reason to spin a racket over a fun match." Oh, well, she thought, I'll just go ahead and slaughter her. Of course, I won't lob over her head, I don't suppose anyone does that to her.

Roxanne pulled the first ball out of her pants. She had a disconcerting habit of sticking the extra ball up the leg of her tights instead of keeping it in a pocket. She pulled the ball out of her pants, tossed it expertly up into the air, and served an ace to LaGrande's extreme backhand service corner.

"Nice serve," LaGrande said. Oh, well, she thought, everyone gets one off occasionally. Let her go on and get overconfident. Then I can get this over in a hurry.

They changed courts for the second serve. Roxanne hit short into the backhand court. LaGrande raced up and hit a forehand right into Roxanne's waiting racket. The ball dropped neatly into a corner and the score was 30-love.

How in the shit did she get to the net so fast, LaGrande thought. Well, I'll have to watch out for that. I thought she was supposed to be crippled.

Roxanne served again, winning the point with a short spinning forehand. Before LaGrande could gather her wits about her she had lost the first game.

Things went badly with her serve and she lost the second game. While she was still recovering from that she lost the third game. Calm down, she told herself. Get hold of yourself. Keep your eye on the ball. Anticipate her moves. It's only because I didn't have a chance to warm up. I'll get going in a minute.

Old Claiborne stood watching the match from a secluded spot near the door to the dining room, watching it with his heart in his throat, not daring to move any farther out onto the balcony for fear he might distract LaGrande and make things worse.

Why doesn't she lob, Claiborne thought. Why in the name of God doesn't she lob? Maybe she thinks she shouldn't do it just because one of that woman's legs is a little bit shorter than the other.

He stood squeezing the Styrofoam cup in his hand. A small hole had developed in the side, and drops of coffee were making a little track down the side of his Fred Perry flannels, but he was oblivious to everything but the action on the court.

He didn't even notice when Nailor came up behind him. Nailor was a haughty old black man who had been with the club since he was a young boy and now was the chief groundskeeper and arbiter of manners among the hired help.

Nailor had spent his life tending Rubico tennis courts without once having the desire to pick up a racket. But he had watched thousands of tennis matches and he knew more about tennis than most players did.

He knew how the little fields of energy that surround men and women move and coalesce and strike and fend off and retreat and attack and conquer. That was what he looked for when he watched tennis. He wasn't interested in the details.

If it was up to Nailor no one but a few select players would ever be allowed to set foot on his Rubico courts. The only time of day when he was really at peace was the half hour from when he finished the courts around 7:15 each morning until they opened the iron gates at 7:45 and the members started arriving.

Nailor had known LaGrande since she came to her father's matches in a perambulator. He had lusted after her ass ever since she got her first white tennis skirt and her first Wilson autograph racket. He had been the first black man to wax her first baby-blue convertible, and he had been taking care of her cars ever since.

Nailor moonlighted at the club polishing cars with a special wax he had invented.

Nailor hated the new members worse than Claiborne did. Ever since the club had moved to its new quarters and they had come crowding in bringing their children and leaving their paper cups all over the courts he had been thinking of retiring.

Now he was watching one of them taking his favorite little missy to the cleaners. She's getting her little booty whipped for sure this morning, he thought. She can't find a place to turn and make a stand. She don't know where to start to stop it. She's got hind teat today whether she likes it or not and I'm glad her daddy's not here to watch it.

Claiborne was oblivious to Nailor. He was trying to decide who would benefit most if he made a show of walking out to the balcony and taking a seat.

He took a chance. He waited until LaGrande's back was to him, then walked out just as Roxanne was receiving serve.

LaGrande made a small rally and won her service, but Roxanne took the next three games for the set. "I don't need to rest between sets unless you do," she said, walking up to the net. "We really haven't been playing that long. I really don't know why I'm playing so well. I guess I'm just lucky today."

"I just guess you are," LaGrande said. "Sure, let's go right on. I've got a date for lunch." Now I'll take her, she thought. Now I'm tired of being polite. Now I'm going to beat the shit out of her.

Roxanne picked up a ball, tossed it into the air, and served another ace into the backhand corner of the forehand court.

Jesus Fucking A Christ, LaGrande thought. She did it again. Where in the name of God did that little Jewish housewife learn that shot.

LaGrande returned the next serve with a lob. Roxanne ran back, caught it on the edge of her racket and dribbled it over the net.

Now LaGrande lost all powers of reason. She began trying to kill the ball on every shot. Before she could get hold of herself she had lost three games, then four, then five, then she was only one game away from losing the match, then only one point.

This is it, LaGrande thought. Armageddon.

Roxanne picked up the balls and served the first one out. She slowed herself down, took a deep breath, tossed up the second ball and shot a clean forehand into the service box.

"Out," LaGrande said. "Nice try."

"It couldn't be out," Roxanne said, "are you sure?"

"Of course I'm sure," LaGrande said. "*I wouldn't have called it unless I was sure.*"

Up on the balcony Old Claiborne's heart was opening and

closing like a geisha's fan. He caught LaGrande's eye, smiled and waved, and, turning around, realized that Nailor was standing behind him.

"Morning, Mr. Claiborne," Nailor said, leaning politely across him to pick up the cup. "Looks like Mr. Leland's baby's having herself a hard time this morning. Let me bring you something nice to drink while you watch."

Claiborne sent him for coffee and settled back in the chair to watch LaGrande finish her off, thinking, as he often did lately, that he had outlived his time and his place. "I'm not suited for a holding action," he told himself, imagining the entire culture of the white Christian world to be stretched out on some sort of endless Maginot Line besieged by the children of the poor carrying portable radios and boxes of fried chicken.

Here Claiborne sat, on a beautiful spring morning, in good spirits, still breathing normally, his blood coursing through his veins on its admirable and accustomed journeys, and only a few minutes before he had been party to a violation of a code he had lived by all his life.

He sat there, sipping his tasteless coffee, listening to the Saturday lawn mowers starting up on the lawn of the Poydras Retirement Home, which took up the other half of the square block of prime New Orleans real estate on which the new clubhouse was built. It was a very exclusive old folks' home, with real antiques and Persian rugs and a board of directors made up of members of the New Orleans Junior League. Some of the nicest old people in New Orleans went there to die.

Claiborne had suffered through a series of terrible luncheons at the Poydras Home in an effort to get them to allow the tennis club to unlock one of the gates that separated the two properties. But no matter how the board of directors of the Lawn Tennis Club pleaded and bargained and implored, the board of directors of the Poydras Home stoutly refused to allow the tennis-club members to set foot on their lawn to retrieve the balls that flew over the fence. A ball lost to the Poydras Home was a ball gone forever.

The old-fashioned steel girders of the Huey P. Long Bridge hung languidly in the moist air. The sun beat down on the river. The low-hanging clouds pushed against each other in fat cosmic orgasms.

LaGrande stood on the bridge until the constellation of yellow balls was out of sight around a bend in the river. Then she drove to her house on Philip Street, changed clothes, got in the car, and began to drive aimlessly up and down Saint Charles Avenue, thinking of things to do with the rest of her life.

She decided to cheer herself up. She turned onto Carrollton Avenue and drove down to Gus Mayer.

She went in, found a saleslady, took up a large dressing room, and bought some cocktail dresses and some sun dresses and some summer skirts and blouses and some pink linen pants and a beige silk Calvin Klein evening jacket.

Then she went downstairs and bought some hose and some makeup and some perfume and some brassieres and some panties and a blue satin Christian Dior gown and robe.

She went into the shoe department and bought some Capezio sandals and some Bass loafers and some handmade espadrilles. She bought a red umbrella and a navy blue canvas handbag.

When she had bought one each of every single thing she could possibly imagine needing she felt better and went on out to the Country Club to see if anyone she liked to fuck was hanging around the pool.

Things Like the Truth

Suicides

Joshua and Philip Treadway were the shining lights of the University of Seattle English Department. They were identical twins, tall, blonde, graceful, brilliant.

They completed each other. Philip was the scholar. Joshua was a musician, the creative, mad, lighthearted brother. He did it first. Did it without saying a word to anyone. Didn't leave a note, not a word of farewell.

Just walked out one night and dumped himself into the Puget Sound. Two witnesses saw him remove his shoes, sit them neatly under an upright, and do a swan dive into the cold, restless water. Not a sign, not a wave. The witnesses stood for a long time, staring down at the spot where he landed, thinking they had been let in on some elaborate practical joke.

Philip made it through the funeral, sleeping across the foot of his mother's bed, trying to be a consolation.

"We'll make it," he told her. "Josh was an artist. You always lose them one way or the other." Philip was the down-to-earth twin, always following Joshua around, picking up his caps and jackets, carrying his extra guitar strings, lending him money.

"But where is the note?" his mother said for the thousandth time. "There must be a note. Surely we'll find the note. What could have happened to the note?"

"We'll stick together," he told his mother. "We'll see each other often. I'll come for weekends." He was saving the good news to tell her later. His wife, Janet, was going to have a baby. There would be new life. It would make a difference.

That was June. In September Philip fell apart. Perhaps it was the beginning of the school year. There he was, with the leaves falling all over the campus, faced with two sections of freshman English, their little, moist, bored faces waiting to be amused.

"How do they seem this year?" Janet asked, handing him a drink, settling beside him on the sofa. She took his hand and placed it on her growing stomach.

"Like visitors from another planet," he said. "Like an army of baby bottles. They stick together. They keep their secrets. Who knows? Perhaps they're harmless. Perhaps they will learn to trust me." He encircled her stomach with his hands. "What will he look like?" he said.

"Like us, of course," she said, touching his soft blonde hair. It was a joke with them, how much they looked alike. With Joshua along they had passed for triplets, in bars, or when they traveled together.

"If only Josh had known about the baby," Philip said. "It might have saved him."

Janet hid her surprise. Joshua had known. They had told him. "It wouldn't have mattered," she said. "Nothing we could have done would have mattered."

"We will name him Joshua," Philip said. "It's the least we can do."

"Of course," she said, glad he was talking about it. "It will be a way of forgiving him."

"He doesn't need forgiving," Philip said, moving away from her. "He knew what he was doing. He had a right to his death. He heard a different music." He was thinking about something Joshua had done, once, when they were apart on their birthday.

The phone began ringing at dawn. When Philip answered it, Joshua was on the other end of the line playing the saxophone, playing wonderful music, playing on and on. Then he hung up, without a word.

Lately, whenever Philip answered the phone, he expected to hear that music.

"Not need forgiving?" Janet said. "How can you say that? After what he's put us through. Look what he's done to your mother... to your father... to you... to me...." She never got to finish the sentence. Philip was gone.

When he showed up three days later he walked into the

den, put a new album on the phonograph, turned it up as loud as it would go, sat down at the dining-room table, and wrote her the first of the letters.

The album was Keith Jarrett's *Death and the Flower*. Philip was through with subtleties.

Dear Bitch,
I have had all I can take of your stupidity. Get rid of the kid. You won't manipulate me with that old trick. Get your fat body out of my bed. Get things cleaned up around here before I burn the place down. If this sounds like a threat, it is.

Softly,
Philip

He tied a necktie into a noose, placed the letter in the knot, and hung it on the refrigerator door.

"Don't worry," the head of the English Department told her. "We'll find him the best doctors. We've been expecting something like this. We were lucky to have a few months' grace. Don't panic. We'll save him. He's our golden boy. And you're our golden girl. Hold on. Help is coming."

Things got better. By the end of the week he fell asleep in her arms, begging forgiveness.

They moved to a new house, a pleasant condominium overlooking a wooded area. There was even a stream nearby, flowing down from the pleasant hills. It would be different now, a new beginning.

Janet rushed around all day, cleaning windows until they squeaked, hanging white curtains, arranging greenery in pots made by their clever friends, cooking thick soups and stews and meat pies.

The baby arrived for Christmas. Philip took one look and disappeared for two weeks. He sent a note with a box of flowers.

Dear Bitch,
The title of this note is WHEN THE CHILD IS BORN THE PARENTS START DYING.
Josh called today. He said it is more beautiful than you could imagine. He said everyone we like to talk to is there. Yeats is there and Thomas. Sylvia is there and

Anne. John is there and Ted and Dylan. Albert and Margaret are there and Blake. Imagine, Blake is there.

Josh wishes he had someone of his own to talk to. You know, someone who really understands him.

Your bosom, your buddy,
Philip

P.S. The baby doesn't like it in the little box. Please have him moved to more suitable quarters.

Janet dropped the letter on the floor beside the hospital bed. She looked out the window at the white landscape. She was all ready to cry. Then a strange thing happened. She raised her hand to her lips and laughter poured out between her fingers.

"It will be all right," everyone said. "Don't panic. It is important not to panic. This was to be expected. It will take some time. It isn't easy."

This time Philip returned with a friend, a huge tangled sheep dog he insisted on keeping in the house although Janet was afraid it might eat the baby. He fed it at the dining-room table, allowed it to sleep on their bed, played his records for it, turning up the speakers until the poor creature howled with pain.

"Truth hurts," Philip said, "truth is very painful."

This time Janet left, taking her books and her baby and fleeing across town to her mother's. The letters grew worse, the threats more terrible.

Dear Bitch,

Who do you think you're fooling? We're onto your game. We're watching every move you make. Remember, the ocean gets hungry. We must keep feeding the ocean. It is very important. Nothing else is important.

Your Philip, your city
of swollen faces

Dear Bitch and Company,

Last night I dreamed you turned the English Department into a cathedral. There were crosses all over the place. There were big crosses and little crosses with real men on them. Very cute. I thought. Then I called the cops. They came and cleaned out the place.

Josh says he loves you. He says he needs you.

Your divine,
Your Philip

She tore up his photographs, applied for a job in New England. She ate a lot of ice cream, gained a lot of weight. She was very lonely. Who would have anything to do with her, embroiled as she was in this tragedy?

This time the reconciliation involved two psychiatrists, a social worker, and the head of the English Department.

"It will work out," they told her. "It's all a balancing act. Intelligent people can solve problems. Man can control his destiny."

They found a small house near Janet's mother. The child was a roly-poly two-year-old. He built elaborate structures out of blocks of wood, knocked them over, stacked the blocks in neat rows, built again, amused himself for hours.

"What an angel," everyone said. "What a beautiful little boy. What a joy to behold, what a reason to live."

It was spring. Sun poured in the windows. Janet went back to work on her paper on Virginia Woolf.

One day for a surprise Philip came home for lunch. He played his records for a while, borrowed some money from her, then went into the bathroom and took all the drugs out of the medicine cabinet.

"We don't need these anymore," he said, stuffing them in a paper bag, "we're through with analgesics." He stuffed in the Seconal and Valium and Empirin #3 with Codeine and the aspirin and Tylenol and Percodan and cough syrup.

He kissed Janet goodbye and walked out toward the car. She stood in the open door with the Keith Jarrett pouring out into the bright crisp April air.

Philip drove down to the hardware store and bought some things he needed. He bought saws and ice picks and hammers and knives and staplers and drills. He bought ice and kerosene and weed killer.

He went by the whiskey store and bought brandy and gin and vodka and bourbon and sherry.

He drove out into the country, into the woods overlooking their old condominium. He drove off the road and along the creek bed until he lodged the Oldsmobile between two birch trees. He trudged back to the road and shoveled dirt on top of the tire tracks and threw the shovel deep into the woods.

Then he went back to the car and went to work on himself. Every now and then he stopped and wrote on the letters.

Dear Joshua,
    Sylvia and Anne and John and Blake and I are waiting... How long will you keep us waiting?

Dear Bitch,
    Don't take this personally. This is just a way of killing time. This is just another way to be creative.

1957, a Romance

It was June in northern Alabama. Upstairs Rhoda's small sons lay sleeping. Somewhere in North Carolina her young husband sulked because she'd left him.

Rhoda had the name. She had fucked her fat, balding gynecologist all Wednesday afternoon to get the name. She had fucked him on the daybed in his office and on the examining table and on the rug in the waiting room. Now all she needed was five hundred dollars.

No one was going to cut Rhoda's stomach open again. She had come home to get help. She had come home to the one person who had never let her down.

She went into the downstairs bathroom, washed her face, and went up to his room to wake him.

"I have to talk to you, Daddy," she said, touching him on the shoulder. "Come downstairs. Don't wake up mother."

They sat down together in the parlor, close together on the little sofa. He was waking up, shaking sleep from his handsome Scotch face. The old T-shirt he wore for a pajama top seemed very dear to Rhoda. She touched it while she talked.

"I have to get some money, Daddy," she said. "I'm pregnant again. I have to have an abortion. I can't stand to have another baby. I'll die if they keep cutting me open. You can't go on having cesarean sections like that."

"Oh, my," he said, his old outfielder's body going very still inside. "Does Malcolm know all this?" Usually he pretended to have forgotten her husband's name.

"No one knows. I have to do this right away, do you understand? I have to do something about it right away."

"You don't want to tell Malcolm?"

"I can't tell Malcolm. He'd never let me do it. I know that.

81

And no one is going to stop me. He got me pregnant on purpose, Daddy. He did it because he knew I was going to leave him sooner or later."

Rhoda was really getting angry. She always believed her own stories as soon as she told them.

"We'll have to find you a doctor, Honey. It's hard to find a doctor that will do that."

"I have a doctor. I have the name of a man in Houston. A Doctor Van Zandt. A friend of mine went to him. Daddy, you have to help me with this. I'm going crazy. Imagine Malcolm doing this to me. He did it to keep me from leaving. . . I begged him not to."

"Oh, Honey," he said. "Please don't tell me all that now. I can't stand to hear all that. It doesn't matter. All that doesn't matter. We have to take care of you now. Let me think a minute."

He put his head down in his hands and conferred with his maker. Well, Sir, he said, I've spoiled her rotten. There's no getting around that. But she's mine and I'm sticking by her. You know I'd like to kill that little son of a bitch with my bare hands but I'll keep myself from doing it. So you help us out of this. You get us out of this one and I'll buy you a stained-glass window with nobody's name on it, or a new roof for the vestry if you'd rather.

Rhoda was afraid he'd gone back to sleep. "It's not my fault, Daddy," she said. "He made me do it. He did it to me on purpose. He did it to keep me from leaving. . ."

"All right, Honey," he said. "Don't think about any of that anymore. I'll take care of it. I'll call your Uncle James in the morning and check up on the doctor. We'll leave tomorrow as soon as I got things lined up."

"You're going with me," she said.

"Of course I'm going with you," he said. "We'll leave your mother with the babies. But, Rhoda, we can't tell your mother about this. I'll tell her I'm taking you to Tennessee to see the mines."

"It costs *five hundred dollars*, Daddy."

"I know that. Don't worry about that. You quit worrying about everything now and go on and try to get some sleep. I'm taking care of this. And, Rhoda. . ."

"Yes?"

"I really don't want your mother to know about this. She's got a lot on her mind right now. And she's not going to like this one bit."

"All right, Daddy. I don't want to tell her, anyway. Daddy, I could have a legal abortion if Malcolm would agree to it. You know that, don't you? People aren't supposed to go on having cesarean sections one right after the other. I know I could get a legal abortion. But you have to have three doctors sign the paper. And that takes too long. It might be too late by the time I do all that. And, besides, Malcolm would try to stop me. I can't take a chance on that. I think he wants to kill me."

"It's all right, Honey. I'm going to take care of it. You go to bed and get some sleep."

Rhoda watched him climb the stairs, sliding his hand along the polished stair rail, looking so vulnerable in his cotton pajama bottoms and his old T-shirt, with his broad shoulders and his big head and his tall, courteous body.

He had been a professional baseball player until she was born. He had been famous in the old Southern League, playing left field for the Nashville Volunteers.

There was a scrapbook full of his old clippings. Rhoda and her brothers had worn it out over the years. DUDLEY MANNING HITS ONE OVER THE FENCE; MANNING DOES IT AGAIN; DUDLEY LEADS THE LEAGUE.

You couldn't eat headlines in the 1930s, so when Rhoda was born he had given in to her mother's pleadings, quit baseball, and gone to work to make money.

He had made money. He had made 2 million dollars by getting up at four o'clock every morning and working his ass off every single day for years. And he had loved it, loved getting up before the sun rose, loved eating his quiet lonely breakfasts, loved learning to control his temper, loved being smarter and better and luckier than everyone else.

Every day he reminded himself that he was the luckiest son of a bitch in the world. And that made him humble, and other men loved him for his humility and forgave him for his success. Taped to his dresser mirror was a little saying he had cut out of a newspaper, "EVERY DAY THE WORLD TURNS UPSIDE DOWN ON SOMEONE WHO THOUGHT THEY WERE SITTING ON TOP OF IT."

He was thinking of the saying as he went back to bed. As long as nothing happens to her, he told himself. As long as she is safe.

Breakfast was terrible. Rhoda picked at her food, pretending to eat, trying to get her mother in a good mood. Her mother, whose name was Jeannie, was a gentle, religious woman who lived her life in service to her family and friends. But she had spells of fighting back against the terrible inroads they made into her small personal life. This was one of those spells.

This was the third time in two years that Rhoda had run away from her husband and come home to live. Jeannie suspected that all Rhoda really wanted was someone to take care of her babies. Jeannie spent a lot of time suspecting Rhoda of one thing or another. Rhoda was the most demanding of her four children, the only daughter, the most unpredictable, the hardest to control or understand.

"What am I supposed to tell your husband when he calls," she said, buttering toast with a shaking hand. "I feel sorry for him when he calls up. If you're leaving town I want you to call him first."

"Now, Jeannie," Rhoda's father said. "We'll only be gone a few days. Don't answer the phone if you don't want to talk to Malcolm."

"I had an appointment to get a *permanent* today," she said. "I don't know when Joseph will be able to take me again."

"Leave the children with the maids," he said. "That's what the maids are for."

"I'm not going to leave those babies alone in a house with maids for a minute," her mother said. "This is just like you, Rhoda, coming home brokenhearted one day and going off leaving your children the next. I don't care what anyone says, Dudley, she has to learn to accept some responsibility for something."

"She's going with me to the mines," he said, getting up and putting his napkin neatly into his napkin holder. "I want her to see where the money comes from."

"Well, I'll call and see if Laura'll come over while I'm gone," Jeannie said, backing down as she always did. Besides, she loved Rhoda's little boys, loved to hold their beautiful strong bodies in her arms, loved to bathe and dress and feed them, to read to them and make them laugh and watch them play. When she was alone with them she forgot they were not her very own. Flesh of my flesh, she would think, touching their perfect skin, which was the color of apricots and wild honey, flesh of my flesh, bone of my bone.

"Oh, go on then," she said. "But please be back by Saturday."

They cruised out of town in the big Packard he had bought secondhand from old Dr. Purcell and turned onto the Natchez Trace going north.

"Where are we going?" she said.

"We have to go to Nashville to catch a plane," he said. "It's too far to drive. Don't worry about it, Honey. Just leave it to me. I've got all my ducks in a row."

"Did you call the doctor?" she said. "Did you call Uncle James?"

"Don't worry about it. I told you I've got it all taken care of. You take a nap or something."

"All right," she said, and pulled a book out of her handbag. It was Ernest Hemingway's new book, and it had come from the book club the day she left North Carolina. She had been waiting for it to come for weeks. Now she opened it to the first page, holding it up to her nose and giving it a smell.

"*Across the River and into the Trees*," she said. "What a wonderful title. Oh, God, he's my favorite writer." She settled further down into the seat. "This is going to be a good one. I can tell."

"Honey, look out the window at where you're going," her father said. "This is beautiful country. Don't keep your nose in a book all your life."

"This is a new book by Ernest Hemingway," she said. "I've been waiting for it for weeks."

"But look at this country," he said. "Your ancestors came this way when they settled this country. This is how they came from Tennessee."

"They did not," she said. "They came on a boat down the river from Pennsylvania. Momma said so."

"Well, I knew you'd have something smart-alecky to say," he said.

"The first book I read by Ernest Hemingway was last year when I was nursing Bobby," she said. "It was about this man and woman in Paris that loved each other but something was wrong with him, he got hurt in the war and couldn't make love to her. Anyway, she kept leaving him and going off with other men. It was so sad I cried all night after I read it. After that I read all his books as fast as I could."

"I don't know why you want to fill up your head with all that stuff," he said. "No wonder you don't have any sense, Rhoda."

"Well, never mind that," she said. "Oh, good, this is really going to be good. It's dedicated 'To Mary, With Love,' that's his wife. She's terrible looking. She doesn't wear any makeup and she's got this terrible wrinkled skin from being in the sun all the time. I saw a picture of her in a magazine last year. I don't know what he sees in her."

"Maybe she knows how to keep her mouth shut," he said. "Maybe she knows how to stay home and be a good wife."

"Oh, well," Rhoda said, "let's don't talk about that. I don't feel like talking about that."

"I'm sorry, Honey," he said. "You go on and read your book." He set the speedometer on an easy sixty miles an hour and tried not to think about anything. Outside the window the hills of north Alabama were changing into the rich fields of Tennessee. He remembered coming this way as a young man, driving to Nashville to play ball, dreaming of fame, dreaming of riches. He glanced beside him, at the concentrated face of his beautiful spoiled crazy daughter.

Well, she's mine, he told himself. And nothing will ever hurt her. As long as I live nothing will ever harm her.

He sighed, letting out his breath in a loud exhalation, but Rhoda could not hear him now. She was far away in the marshes near Tagliamento, in northern Italy, hunting ducks at dawn with Ernest Hemingway. (Rhoda was not fooled by personas. In her mind any modern novel was the true story of the writer's life.)

Rhoda was reading as they went into the Nashville airport and she kept on reading while they waited for the plane, and as soon as she was settled in her seat she found her place and went on reading.

The love story had finally started. "*Then she came into the room, shining in her youth and tall striding beauty, and the carelessness the wind had made of her hair. She had pale, almost olive colored skin, a profile that could break your, or anyone else's heart, and her dark hair, of a thick texture, hung down over her shoulders.*

'Hello, my great beauty,' the Colonel said."

This was more like it, Rhoda thought. This was a better girlfriend for Ernest Hemingway than his old wife. She read on. Renata was nineteen! Imagine that! Ernest Hemingway's girlfriend was the same age as Rhoda! Imagine being in Venice with a wonderful old writer who was about to die of a heart attack. Imagine making love to a man like that. Rhoda imagined herself in a wonderful bed in a hotel in Venice making love all night to a dying author who could fuck like a nineteen-year-old boy.

She raised her eyes from the page. "Did you get Uncle James on the phone?" she said. "Did you ask him to find out about the doctor?"

"He told me what to do," her father said. "He said first you should make certain you're pregnant."

"I'm certain," she said. "I even know why. A rubber broke. It was Malcolm's birthday and I was out of jelly and I told him I didn't want to . . ."

"Oh, Honey, please don't talk like that. Please don't tell me all that."

"Well, it's the truth," she said. "It's the reason we're on this plane."

"Just be quiet and go on and read your book then," he said. He went back to his newspaper. In a minute he decided to try again.

"James said the doctor will have to know for certain that you're pregnant."

"All right," she said. "I'll think up something to tell him. What do you think we should say my name is?"

"Now, Sweetie, don't start that," he said. "We're going to tell this man the truth. We're not doing anything we're ashamed of."

"Well, we can't tell him I'm married," she said. "Or else he'll make me get my husband's permission."

"Where'd you get an idea like that?" he said.

"Stella Mabry told me. She tried to get an abortion last year, but she didn't take enough money with her. You have to say you're divorced."

"All right," he said. "I'll tell you what, Honey. You just let me talk to the man. You be quiet and I'll do the talking."

He lay back and closed his eyes, hoping he wasn't going to end up vomiting into one of Southern Airlines' paper bags.

He was deathly afraid to fly and had only been on an airplane once before in his life.

A taxi took them to the new Hilton. Rhoda had never been in such a fancy hotel. She had run away to get married when she was seventeen years old and her only vacations since then had been to hospitals to have babies.

The bellboy took them upstairs to a suite of rooms. There were two bedrooms and a large living room with a bar in one corner. It looked like a movie set, with oversize beige sofas and a thick beige tweed carpet. Rhoda looked around approvingly and went over to the bar and fixed herself a tall glass of ice water.

Her father walked out onto the balcony and called to her. "Rhoda, look out here. That's an Olympic-size swimming pool. Isn't that something? The manager said some Olympic swimmers had been working out here in the afternoons. Maybe we'll get to watch them after a while."

She looked down several stories to the bright blue rectangle. "Can I go swimming in it?" she said.

"Let's call the doctor first and see what he wants us to do." He took a phone number from his billfold, sat down in a chair with his back to her, and talked for a while on the phone, nodding his head up and down as he talked.

"He said to come in first thing in the morning. He gets there at nine."

"Then I'll go swimming until dinner," she said.

"Fine," he said. "Did you bring a swimsuit?"

"Oh, no," she said. "I didn't think about it."

"Well, here," he said, handing her a hundred dollar bill. "Go find a gift shop and see if they don't have one that will fit you. And buy a robe to go over it. You can't go walking around a hotel in a swimsuit. I'll take a nap while you're gone. I'll come down and find you later."

She went down to the ground floor and found the gift shop, a beautiful little glassed-in area that smelled of cool perfume and was presided over by an elegant woman with her hair up in a bun.

Rhoda tried on five or six swimming suits and finally settled on a black one-piece maillot cut low in the back. She admired herself in the mirror. Two weeks of being too worried to eat had melted the baby fat from her hips and stomach, and she was pleased with the way her body looked.

While she admired herself in the mirror the saleslady handed her a beach robe. It was a black-and-white geometric print that came down to the floor.

"This is the latest thing in the Caribbean," the saleslady said. "It's the only one I have left. I sold one last week to a lady from New York."

"It's darling," Rhoda said, wrapping it around her, imagining what Ernest Hemingway would think if he could see her in this. "But it's too long."

"How about a pair of Wedgies," the saleslady said. "I've got some on sale.

Rhoda added a pair of white canvas Wedgies to her new outfit, collected the clothes she had been wearing in a shopping bag, paid for her purchases, and went out to sit by the pool.

The swimming team had arrived and was doing warm-up laps. A waiter came, and she ordered a Coke and sipped it while she watched the beautiful young bodies of the athletes. There was a blonde boy whose shoulders reminded her of her husband's and she grew interested in him, wondering if he was a famous Olympic swimmer. He looked like he would be a lot of fun, not in a bad mood all the time like Malcolm. She kept looking at him until she caught his eye and he smiled at her. When he dove back into the pool she reached under the table and took off her wedding ring and slipped it into her pocketbook.

When she woke up early the next morning her father was already up, dressed in a seersucker suit, talking on the phone to his mine foreman in Tennessee.

"I can't believe I'm going to be through with all this today," she said, giving him a kiss on the forehead. "I love you for doing this for me, Daddy. I won't ever forget it as long as I live."

"Well, let's just don't talk about it too much," he said. "Here, look what's in the paper. Those sapsuckers in Washington are crazy as loons. We haven't been through with Korea four years and they're fixing to drag us into this mess in Vietnam. Old Douglas MacArthur told them not to get into a land war in Asia, but nobody would listen to him."

"Let me see," Rhoda said, taking the newspaper from him. She agreed with her father that the best way to handle foreign affairs was for the United States to divide up the world with Russia. "They can boss half and we'll boss half," he had been preaching for years. "Because that's the way it's going to end up anyway."

Rhoda's father was in the habit of being early to his appointments, so at eight o'clock they descended in the elevator, got into a taxi, and were driven through the streets of Houston to a tall office building in the center of town. They went up to the fifth floor and into a waiting room that looked like any ordinary city doctor's office. There was even a Currier and Ives print on the wall. Her father went in and talked to the doctor for a while, then he came to the door and asked her to join them. The doctor was a short, nervous man with thin light-colored hair and a strange smell about him. Rhoda thought he smelled like a test tube. He sat beside an old rolltop desk and asked her questions, half-listening to the answers.

"I'm getting a divorce right away," Rhoda babbled, "my husband forced me to make love to him and I'm not supposed to have any more babies because I've already had two cesarean sections in twelve months and I could have a legal abortion if I wanted to but I'm afraid to wait as long as it would take to get permission. I mean I'm only nineteen and what would happen to my babies if I died. Anyway, I want you to know I think you're a real humanitarian for doing this for people. I can't tell you what it meant to me to even find out your name. Do you remember Stella Mabry that came here last year? Well, anyway, I hope you're going to do this for me because I think I'll just go crazy if you don't."

90

"Are you sure you're pregnant?" he asked.

"Oh, yes," she said. "I'm sure. I've missed a period for three and a half weeks and I've already started throwing up. That's why I'm so sure. Look, I just had two babies in thirteen months. I know when I'm pregnant. Look at the circles under my eyes. And I've been losing weight. I always lose weight at first. Then I blow up like a balloon." Oh, God, she thought. Please let him believe me. Please make him do it.

"And another thing," she said. "I don't care what people say about you. I think you are doing a great thing. There will be a time when everyone will know what a great service you're performing. I don't care what anyone says about what you're doing. . . "

"Honey," her father said. "Just answer his questions."

"When was your last period," the doctor said. He handed her a calendar and she picked out a date and pointed to it.

Then he gave her two small white pills to swallow and a nurse came and got her and helped her undress and she climbed up on an operating table and everything became very still and dreamy and the nurse was holding her hand. "Be still," the nurse said. "It won't take long."

She saw the doctor between her parted legs with a mask tied around his face and an instrument in his hand and she thought for a moment he might be going to kill her, but the nurse squeezed her hand and she looked up at the ceiling and thought of nothing but the pattern of the tiles revolving around the light fixture.

They began to pack her vagina with gauze. "Relax," the nurse said. "It's all over."

"I think you are wonderful," she said in a drowsy voice. "I think you are a wonderful man. I don't care what anyone says about you. I think you are doing a great service to mankind. Someday everyone will know what a good thing you're doing for people."

When she woke up her father was with her and she walked in a dream out of the offices and into the elevator and down to the tiled foyer and out onto the beautiful streets of the city. The sun was brilliant and across the street from the office building was a little park with the sound of a million crickets rising and falling in the sycamore trees. And all the time a song was playing inside of her. "I don't have to have a baby, I don't have to have a baby, I don't have to have a baby."

"Oh, God, oh, thank you so much," she said, leaning against her father. "Oh, thank you, oh, thank you so much. Oh, thank you, thank you, thank you."

He took her to the hotel and put her into the cool bed and covered her with blankets and sat close beside her in a chair all afternoon and night while she slept. The room was dark and cool and peaceful, and whenever she woke up he was there beside her and nothing could harm her ever as long as he lived. No one could harm her or have power over her or make her do anything as long as he lived.

All night he was there beside her, in his strength and goodness, as still and gentle as a woman.

All night he was there, half-asleep in his chair. Once in the night she woke up hungry and room service brought a steak and some toast and milk and he fed it to her bite by bite. Then he gave her another one of the pills, put the glass of milk to her lips, and she drank deeply of the cold, lush liquid, then fell back into a dreamless sleep.

The plane brought them to Nashville by noon the next day, and they got into the Packard and started driving home.

He had made a bed for her in the back seat with pillows for her head and his raincoat for a cover and she rode along that way, sleeping and reading her book. The wad of gauze in her vagina was beginning to bother her. It felt like a thick hand inside her body. The doctor had said she could remove it in twenty-four hours, but she was afraid to do it yet.

Well, at least that's over, she thought. At least I don't have to have any more babies this year.

All I have to do is have one more and they'll give me a tubal ligation. Doctor Greer promised me that. On the third cesarean section you get to have your tubes cut. It's a law. They have to do it. It would be worth having another baby for that. Oh, well, she thought. At least I don't have to worry about it anymore for now. She opened her book.

"*You are not that kind of soldier and I am not that kind of girl,*" Renata was saying to Colonel Cantrell. "*But sometime give me something lasting that I can wear and be happy each time I wear it.*"

92

"I see," the Colonel said, "And I will."

"You learn fast about things you do not know," the girl said. "And you make lovely quick decisions. I would like you to have the emeralds and you could keep them in your pocket like a lucky piece, and feel them if you were lonely."

Rhoda fell asleep, dreaming she was leaning across a table staring into Ernest Hemingway's eyes as he lit her cigarette.

When they got to the edge of town he woke her. "How are you feeling, Honey," he said. "Do you feel all right?"

"Sure," she said. "I feel great, really I do."

"I want to go by the house on Manley Island if you feel like it," he said. "Everyone's out there."

It's the Fourth of July, she thought. I had forgotten all about it. Every year her father's large Scotch family gathered for the fourth on a little peninsula that jutted out into the Tennessee River a few miles from town.

"Will Jamie be there?" she asked. Jamie was everyone's favorite. He was going to be a doctor like his father.

"I think so. Do you feel like going by there?"

"Of course I do," she said. "Stop and let me get into the front seat with you."

They drove up into a yard full of automobiles. The old summer house was full of cousins and aunts and uncles, all carrying drinks and plates of fried chicken and all talking at the same time.

Rhoda got out of the car feeling strange and foreign and important, as if she were a visitor from another world, arriving among her kinfolk carrying an enormous secret that they could not imagine, not even in their dreams.

She began to feel terribly elated, moving among her cousins, hugging and kissing them.

Then her Uncle James came and found her. He was an eye surgeon. Her father had paid his tuition to medical school when there was barely enough money to feed Rhoda and her brothers.

"Let's go for a walk and see if any of Cammie's goats are still loose in the woods," he said, taking hold of her arm.

"I'm fine," she said. "I'm perfectly all right, Uncle James."

"Well, just come walk with me and tell me about it," he said. They walked down the little path that led away from the

93

house to the wild gardens and orchards at the back of the property. He had his hand on her arm. Rhoda loved his hands, which were always unbelievably clean and smelled wonderful when they came near you.

"Tell me about it," he said.

"There isn't anything to tell," she said. "They put me up on an examining table and first they gave me some pills and they made me sleepy and they said it might hurt a little but it didn't hurt and I slept a long time afterwards. Well, first we went down in an elevator and then we went back to the hotel and I slept until this morning. I can't believe that was only yesterday."

"Have you been bleeding?"

"Not a lot. Do you think I need some penicillin? He was a real doctor, Uncle James. There were diplomas on the wall and a picture of his family. What about the penicillin? Should I take it just in case?"

"No, I think you're going to be fine. I'm going to stay around for a week just in case."

"I'm glad you came. I wanted to see Jamie. He's my favorite cousin. He's getting to be so handsome. I'll bet the girls are crazy about him."

"Tell me this," he said. "Did the doctor do any tests to see if you were pregnant?"

"I know I was pregnant," she said. "I was throwing up every morning. Besides, I've been pregnant for two years. I guess I know when I'm pregnant by now."

"You didn't have tests made?"

"How could I? I would have had to tell somebody. Then they might have stopped me."

"I doubt if you were really pregnant," he said. "I told your father I think it's highly unlikely that you were really pregnant."

"I know I was pregnant."

"Rhoda, listen to me. You don't have any way of knowing that. The only way you can be sure is to have the tests and it would be doing your father a big favor if you told him you weren't sure of it. I think you imagined you were pregnant because you dread it so much."

Rhoda looked at his sweet impassive face trying to figure out what he wanted from her, but the face kept all its secrets.

94

"Well, it doesn't matter to me whether I was or not,'· she said. "All I care about is that it's over. Are you sure I don't need any penicillin? I don't want to get blood poisoning."

(Rhoda was growing tired of the conversation. It isn't any of his business what I do, she thought, even if he is a doctor.)

She left him then and walked back to the house, glancing down every now and then at her flat stomach, running her hand across it, wondering if Jamie would like to take the boat up to Guntersville Dam to go through the locks.

Her mother had arrived from town with the maid and her babies and she went in and hugged them and played with them for a minute, then she went into the bathroom and gingerly removed the wad of bloody gauze and put in a tampon.

She washed her legs and rubbed hand lotion on them and then she put on the new black bathing suit. It fit better than ever.

"I'm beautiful," she thought, running her hands over her body. "I'm skinny and I'm beautiful and no one is ever going to cut me open. I'm skinny and I'm beautiful and no one can make me do anything."

She began to laugh. She raised her hand to her lips and great peals of clear abandoned laughter poured out between her fingers, filling the tiny room, laughing back at the wild excited face in the bright mirror.

Generous Pieces

I am poking around the house looking for change to spend at the Sweet Shoppe. It is afternoon, November. The light coming through the windows of my parents' room is flat and gray and casts thick shadows on the rug my father brought home from China after the war.

I am going through the pockets of his gabardine topcoat. The pockets are deep and cool. The rubbers are in the right-hand pocket. I pull them out, look at them for a moment, then stick my hand back in the pocket and leave it there. I stand like that for a long time, halfway into the closet with my hand deep in the pocket, listening to the blood run through my body, to the sound of my own breathing.

I smell the cold safety of his suits and shirts. I stare down at the comforting order of his shoes and boots. I hold one of the little packets between my fingers, feeling the hard rim, the soft yielding center. It gives way, like the hide of a mouse.

Behind me is the walnut bed in which he was born far away in Georgia. Beside it, the old-fashioned dresser with a silver tray onto which he empties his pockets in the evenings. While he dreams the tray holds his daytime life, his plumb bob, his pocketknife, his pens and pencils, his onyx Kappa Sigma ring, his loose change, his money clip.

How do I know what the rubbers are? How do I know with such absolute certainty that they are connected with Christina Carver's mother and the pall that has fallen over our house on Calvin Boulevard?

I stand in the closet door for a long time. I want to take out the little package and inspect it more closely, but I cannot bring myself to withdraw it from the pocket, as if to pull it out into the light would make it real. After a while I become afraid my mother will come home and find me in her room so I take my hand from the pocket and leave.

I wander into the kitchen and make a sugar sandwich and talk for a while to the elderly German housekeeper. She is a kindly woman with a thick accent who smiles all the time. She has a small grandson who is deaf, and occasionally she brings him to work and talks with him in the language deaf people make with their hands. I feel sorry for her because of the deaf child and try to remember to pick up my clothes so she won't have to bend over to reach them. When I am good about this she bakes me gingerbread men with buttons and smiles made out of raisins.

I leave the house and begin walking aimlessly across the small Indiana town. Usually I go by Christina's after school. We are best friends. We spend the night together on weekends. We stand by each other in lines. I work hard to make Christina my friend. I need her for an ally as we have only lived in this town six months and she is the most popular girl in the class.

We have lived in five towns in three years. Every time we move my father makes more money. Every place we live we have a nicer house. This time we are not going to move anymore he promises. This time we are going to stay put.

I want to stay put. When the junior-high cheerleader elections are held in the spring the girls will try out in pairs. If I try out with Christina I know I will win.

My mother was a cheerleader at the University of Georgia. Her senior year in college she was voted Most Popular Girl. There is a full-page photograph of her in the 1929 University of Georgia yearbook. She is wearing a handmade lace dress the color of snow, the color of marble. Her face is small and sweet and full of sadness. Underneath her feet in black letters it says, *Most Popular Girl*.

I will never be popular. But at least I can get elected cheerleader. I do Christina's homework. I write her book reports. I carry messages to her secret boyfriend. He is a college boy named Dawson who plays the saxophone and is dying of cancer in an apartment behind his Jewish grandmother's mansion. I carry their messages. I stand guard when she goes to visit him. I listen to her love stories. They lie down together on a bed with their clothes on and strange things happen. One thing they do is called dryfucking. I don't really understand what it is but I feel funny and excited when she talks about it.

Once I went with her to Dawson's apartment, some rooms above a brick garage of the only mansion in Seymour, Indiana. There were phonograph albums and cartoons nailed to the walls. Dawson was very nice to me. He kept making me listen to something called *Jazz at the Philharmonic*. I pretended to like it. I pretended to like the worst part of all when someone named JoJo plays the drums for about fifteen minutes.

I pass the grade school and turn onto Duncan Street where Christina has lived every day of her life. Next door to her house is a vacant lot. A bicycle I used to own is rusting in a corner of the lot. It has a flat tire but I have never bothered walking it to the service station to get it fixed. I have a new bicycle with shiny fenders. Christina's mother always teases me about the old bike. "It must be nice to be rich," she says, laughing.

She thinks it is funny that no one makes me do anything about it. Christina has to do all kinds of things my mother would never dream of making me do. She has to help with the dishes and iron her own clothes and practice the piano for an hour every day and go horseback riding on Saturday.

When I get to Christina's house she is in the dining room with her mother looking at the fabrics they have spread out all over the dining room table. They have been to a sale and the dining room table is covered with bright plaid wools and gold and blue corduroy and a heavy quilted cotton with little flowers on a green background.

"Here's Margaret now," her mother says, smiling at me, moving closer, her small, brisk body making me feel heavy and awkward and surprised. "Margaret, look at these bargains we got at Hazard's. We're going to make skirts and weskits. Look, we bought something for you. So you and Christina can have twin outfits." She holds up the quilted fabric. "Isn't it darling? Isn't it the darlingest thing you've ever seen?"

She is always so gay, so full of plans. I think of her getting into the Packard with my father the night they went off to

Benton to the ballgame, the night my mother wouldn't go. Christina's father was out of town and I stood on the porch watching my father put her into his big car. My mother stood in the dark doorway not saying a word and later she went into the bedroom and locked the door. My mother has not been well lately. She is worn out. She has hot flashes. She takes hormones and writes long letters to Mississippi and is always mad at me.

"Do you like it?" Christina's mother says, holding the fabric against her body as if she were a model.

"Oh, my," I say, taking the material. "I love it. It's darling. Is it really for me?"

"Look," Christina says, "the one with the green background is for you, to go with your red hair. We got the same print with a blue background for me. Won't we look great together? You aren't supposed to mix blue and green together but who cares. We can wear them to the Christmas Follies if we get them made in time."

"You're going to *make* it for me?" I say.

"Of course we are," her mother says. "I'll get started on it tomorrow morning. I can't wait to see how cute you'll look together. Besides I need to do something to pay your father back for all the help he's been to us with our taxes. I'll have to measure you first, though. Can I do it now?"

"I can't stay that long today," I say quickly, not wanting her to know how big my waist is. It is twenty-six. I will never be a belle. "I'll come back tomorrow and let you do it, if that's O.K."

"Whenever you have time," she says. "I can go on and start on Christina's."

Christina walks me out into the yard. "She's going to a horse show on Saturday," she says. "Do you want to go with me to see Dawson?"

"Sure," I say.

"I don't know what I'd do without you," Christina says. "I don't know what I did before you moved here. Dawson says you're darling. He thinks you're smart as a whip. He wants you to come back over. He wants you to meet a friend of his from college."

"I'll see you tomorrow then," I say. "I'll come by in the

morning. And thanks a lot about the skirt. That's really nice of your mother."

I walk off down Duncan Street for a few blocks, then change my mind about going home. I decide to walk out toward the railroad tracks and get some exercise to make myself smaller before I get measured.

It will be light for another hour. I think about going by Janet Ingram's house to see what she is doing. Janet lives on the edge of town in a house that is very different from the ones Christina and I live in. There are stained red carpets on the floors and over the mantel is a collection of china bulls her father wins at carnivals. I know I am not supposed to go there although my mother has never actually told me so.

Janet's father sleeps in the daytime and works at night in a factory. Once I was there in the afternoon and he was just getting up, walking around the house in a sleeveless T-shirt. I walk along, thinking about the way Janet's house smells, warm and close and foreign, as though the air were full of germs.

I try not to think about Christina's mother. If I think of her I remember how she leans over my father's chair handing him things when they have dinner at our house. I think of him putting her into his car. Then I think of the beautiful quilted material. I think of Christina and me walking into the junior high together, wearing our matching outfits.

I am walking along a new street where houses are under construction. Two men are still hammering on the high beams of one. They are standing on the slanting half-finished roof. I am afraid they will fall while I am watching them and I turn my face away. It is terrible for people to have dangerous jobs like that. I'm glad my father doesn't have a dangerous job. People who are poor have to have jobs like that. Perhaps it doesn't matter as much what happens to them.

Janet comes to the door. Her father is in the living room putting on his shoes. "I can't ask you to stay," she says. "My dad's getting ready to leave for work and I have to help with dinner."

"That's all right," I say. "I was just walking around. I just came by to see what you were doing."

I am staring at Janet's breasts, which are even larger than mine. I wonder if it is true that Janet lets boys touch her breasts.

I begin walking home. Dark is falling faster than I expected. The days grow shorter. It is almost Thanksgiving.

A group of children playing in a yard begins following me. One of them recognizes me from school. He picks up a dirt clod and throws it at me. It hits my coat. I don't know what to do. No one has ever thrown anything at me before. I look up. Another dirt clod hits me on the shoulder. I begin to run, trying to figure out what is going on. I run through the darkening streets as fast as I can. Streetlights flicker and come on. Here and there a yellow porch light shines brightly. I run and run, afraid of falling down, afraid of every shadow, afraid to look up, afraid of the trees, afraid of the moon.

Now it is full dark. How did it get dark so quickly? I fear the dark. I never sleep without a light in my room. If I wake in the night in the dark I am terrified and jump out of bed and run down to my parents' room and tremble between them until morning.

The night is so still I can hear the branches of the trees reaching out their arms for me. A huge moon has appeared in the eastern sky. I run past the construction site. The exposed beams stand out against the dark blue sky. I think if I looked inside I would find the bodies of the carpenters broken and bleeding on the floor.

I run past an alley where I found an automatic card shuffler in a trashcan once when my grandmother was visiting us. When I brought it home she flew into hysterics and bathed me with lye soap, lecturing me about diseases I could catch from strangers.

Now I am on my own street. I run past the Dustins' house. I run into my house and down the hall and turn around and around and run into the kitchen and find my father sitting at the table with my brother. They are laughing and cutting fat green olives into generous pieces.

I throw myself upon him screaming, "Look what they did to me! Look what they did to me! Look what they did!"

He takes me into the bedroom and sits on the bed with

me. He holds me in his arms. My face is against his shirt. I burrow into the strength of his body. Once I look up and there are tears running down his cheeks.

My mother is touching my hair. "It's from living like this," she says. "This insane life in this hick Yankee town. I don't know who she's with half the time. God knows who she plays with. God knows what she's doing."

"What do you want me to do?" he says. "Go home and starve in Waycross? Run a hardware store the rest of my life?"

"I don't know," she says. "I don't know what I want you to do."

After a while my mother undresses me and puts me in bed in her soft flowered nightgown. She brings me a hot toddy and feeds it to me with a spoon. The hot liquor runs down my throat and soothes me. My mother promises to stay with me till I sleep. She turns off the lamp. She sits touching my arm with her soft hands. And the terror draws in its white arms and is still, watching me with cold eyes from the mirror on my father's dresser.

Indignities

Last night my mother took off her clothes in front of twenty-six invited guests in the King's Room at Antoine's. She took off her Calvin Klein evening jacket and her beige silk wrap-around blouse and her custom-made brassiere and walked around the table letting everyone look at the place where her breasts used to be.

She had had them removed without saying a word to anyone. I'm surprised she told my father. I'm surprised she invited him to the party. He never would have noticed. He hasn't touched her in years except to hand her a check or a paper to sign.

After mother took off her blouse the party really warmed up. Everyone stayed until the restaurant closed. Teddy Lanier put the make on a waiter. Alice Lemle sang "A Foggy Day in London Town." A poet called Cherokee stood up on an antique chair, tore open her dress, and drew the sign for infinity on her chest with a borrowed Flair pen. Amalie DuBois sat down by the baked Alaska and began eating the meringue with her fingers.

Everyone followed us home. Someone opened the bar and Clarence Josephy sat down at the baby grand and began improvising. He always makes himself at home. There was a terrible period in my childhood when I thought he was going to be my father. I started going to mass with a little girl from Sacred Heart to pray he wouldn't move in and have breakfast with us every day. I even bought a crucifix. I had worked up to forty-six Hail Marys a day by the time my father came home from Australia and the crisis passed.

As soon as everyone was settled with a drink mother went

upstairs to change and I followed her. "Well, Mother," I said, "this takes the cake. You could have given me some warning. I thought I was coming home for a birthday party."

"I'm leaving it all to you, Melissa," she said. "Take my advice. Sell everything and fly to Paris."

I threw myself down on the bed with my hands over my ears, but she went tirelessly and relentlessly on "This is your chance to rise above the categories," she said. "God knows I've done my best to teach you the relativity of it all." She sighed and shook her head, stepping into a long white dressing gown. I had always been a disappointment to her, that's for certain. No illicit drugs, no unwanted pregnancies, no lesbian affairs, no irate phone calls from teachers, never a moment's doubt that I was living up to my potential.

Melissa was born old, my mother always tells everyone, born with her fingers crossed.

"Why do you think you're dying, Mother?" I said. "Just tell me that, will you? Lots of women get breast cancer. It doesn't mean you're going to die."

"It means I'm going to die," she said. "And I'll tell you one thing. I am never setting foot inside that hospital again. I've never run across such a humorless unimaginative group in my life. And the food! Really, it's unforgivable."

"Mother," I said, trying to put my arms around her.

"Now, Melissa," she said, "let's save the melodrama for the bourgeoisie. I have a book for you to read." She always has a book for me to read. She has a book about everything. She reads the first chapter and the table of contents and the last three paragraphs and if she likes the theory she says APPROVED and goes on to the next book.

If she really likes the theory she writes the author and the publisher and buys twenty copies and gives them away to friends. She has ruined a lot of books for me that way. What real book could live up to one of mother's glowing and inaccurate descriptions?

It must be interesting to be her daughter, people say to me.

I don't know, I tell them. I've never tried it. I use her for a librarian.

The book she pressed upon me now was *Life after Life* by

Raymond A. Moody, Jr., M.D. It was full of first-person accounts by men and women who were snatched from the jaws of death and came back to tell of their ecstatic experiences on the brink of nonbeing. The stories are remarkably similar. It seems the soul lifts off from the body like a sort of transparent angel and floats around the corpse. Then the person sees someone he is dying to talk to standing at the end of a tunnel swinging a lantern and waiting for him.

"But who are you in such a hurry to see, Mother," I said, "all of your friends are downstairs and you never liked your own parents."

"Perhaps Leonardo will be there. Perhaps Blake is waiting for me. Or Margaret Mead or Virginia Woolf."

"How old will you be in heaven, Mother?" I ask, being drawn into the fantasy.

"Oh, thirty-four I think. Attractive, yet intelligent enough to be interesting. What color was my hair at that age? The only thing I regret about all this is that I never had time to grow out my gray hair. I kept putting it off. Vanity, vanity."

"Mother, let's stop this."

"Right. Not another word." She sprayed herself with Shalimar and giving me a pat on the cheek went downstairs to her guests, leaving me alone in her room.

Her room is half of the second floor of a Queen Anne house designed by Thomas Sully in 1890.

There is a round bed on a dais with dozens of small soft pillows piled against a marble headboard. There is a quilt made by her great-grandmother's slaves and linen sheets the colors of the sky at evening.

Everything else in the room is white, white velvet, white satin, white silk, white marble, white painted wood.

There is a dressing table six feet long covered with every product ever manufactured by Charles of the Ritz.

There is a huge desk littered with papers and books, her unpublished poems, her short stories, her journals, her unfinished novels.

"Mother," I called, following her into the hall, "what about the novels. Who will finish the novels?"

"We'll give them to somebody who needs them," she called back. "Some poor person who doesn't have any."

I went downstairs to find her reclining on a love seat with her admirers sitting at her feet drinking brandy and helping plan the funeral.

I was surprised at how traditional her plans have become. Gone was the flag-shaped tombstone saying IT SEEMED LIKE A GOOD IDEA AT THE TIME. Gone the videotape machine in the mausoleum.

"Some readings from García Márquez," she was saying. "Lionel can do them in Spanish. Spanish always sounds so *religious*, don't you agree?"

"How long do you think it will be," Bartlett said.

"Not more than six months surely," mother said. "February."

"I like a winter funeral myself," Eric said. "Especially in this climate."

The weather was perfect for the funeral. "Don't you know she *arranged* this," everyone kept saying. As we were entering the chapel a storm blew up quite suddenly. Rain beat on the walls and lightning flashed through the stained-glass windows.

Then, just as we were carrying the coffin outside, the sun broke from the clouds. "That was going too far," everyone agreed.

Later, a wind blew up from the east and continued to blow while we shoveled dirt on the coffin. "Really!" everyone muttered.

"Melissa," she had said to me, "swear you will never let strangers lower my box." So, while the gravediggers sat politely nearby wondering if we belonged to some new kind of cult, we cranked the coffin down and picked up the shovels.

Clarence turned on the tape player and we shoveled to Mahler for a while, then to Clementi, then Bach.

"I remember the night she chartered a plane and flew to California for the earthquake," Lionel said, pulling a feather out of his hat and dropping it in the hole. He was wearing a velvet suit and an enormous green hat with feathers. He looked like a prehistoric bird.

"Remember the year she learned to scuba dive," Selma said, weeping all over her white tuxedo and dropping an onyx ring on top of the feather. "She didn't even know how to *swim*."

"I remember the week she played with me," I said. "I was four years old. She called and had a piano crate delivered and we turned it into a house and painted murals all over the walls. The title of our mural was Welsh Fertility Rites with Sheepdogs Rampant."

The wind kept on blowing and I kept on shoveling, staring down at all that was left of my childhood, now busily growing out yards and yards of two-toned hair.

Perils of the Nile

Revenge

It was the summer of the Broad Jump Pit.

The Broad Jump Pit, how shall I describe it! It was a bright orange rectangle in the middle of a green pasture. It was three feet deep, filled with river sand and sawdust. A real cinder track led up to it, ending where tall poles for pole-vaulting rose forever in the still Delta air.

I am looking through the old binoculars. I am watching Bunky coming at a run down the cinder path, pausing expertly at the jump-off line, then rising into the air, heels stretched far out in front of him, landing in the sawdust. Before the dust has settled Saint John comes running with the tape, calling out measurements in his high, excitable voice.

Next comes my thirteen-year-old brother, Dudley, coming at a brisk jog down the track, the pole-vaulting pole held lightly in his delicate hands, then vaulting, high into the sky. His skinny tanned legs make a last, desperate surge, and he is clear and over.

Think how it looked from my lonely exile atop the chicken house. I was ten years old, the only girl in a house full of cousins. There were six of us, shipped to the Delta for the summer, dumped on my grandmother right in the middle of a world war.

They built this wonder in answer to a V-Mail letter from my father in Europe. The war was going well, my father wrote, within a year the Allies would triumph over the forces of evil, the world would be at peace, and the Olympic torch would again be brought down from its mountain and carried to Zurich or Amsterdam or London or Mexico City, wher-

111

ever free men lived and worshiped sports. My father had been a participant in an Olympic event when he was young.

Therefore, the letter continued, Dudley and Bunky and Philip and Saint John and Oliver were to begin training. The United States would need athletes now, not soldiers.

They were to train for broad jumping and pole-vaulting and discus throwing, for fifty-, one-hundred-, and four-hundred-yard dashes, for high and low hurdles. The letter included instructions for building the pit, for making pole-vaulting poles out of cane, and for converting ordinary sawhorses into hurdles. It ended with a page of tips for proper eating and admonished Dudley to take good care of me as I was my father's own dear sweet little girl.

The letter came one afternoon. Early the next morning they began construction. Around noon I wandered out to the pasture to see how they were coming along. I picked up a shovel.

"Put that down, Rhoda," Dudley said. "Don't bother us now. We're working."

"I know it," I said. "I'm going to help."

"No, you're not," Bunky said. "This is the Broad Jump Pit. We're starting our training."

"I'm going to do it too," I said. "I'm going to be in training."

"Get out of here now," Dudley said. "This is only for boys, Rhoda. This isn't a game."

"I'm going to dig it if I want to," I said, picking up a shovelful of dirt and throwing it on Philip. On second thought I picked up another shovelful and threw it on Bunky.

"Get out of here, Ratface," Philip yelled at me. "You German spy." He was referring to the initials on my Girl Scout uniform.

"You goddamn niggers," I yelled. "You niggers. I'm digging this if I want to and you can't stop me, you nasty niggers, you Japs, you Jews." I was throwing dirt on everyone now. Dudley grabbed the shovel and wrestled me to the ground. He held my arms down in the coarse grass and peered into my face.

"Rhoda, you're not having anything to do with this Broad

112

Jump Pit. And if you set foot inside this pasture or come around here and touch anything we will break your legs and drown you in the bayou with a crowbar around your neck." He was twisting my leg until it creaked at the joints. "Do you get it, Rhoda? Do you understand me?"

"Let me up," I was screaming, my rage threatening to split open my skull. "Let me up, you goddamn nigger, you Jap, you spy. I'm telling Grannie and you're going to get the worst whipping of your life. And you better quit digging this hole for the horses to fall in. Let me up, let me up. Let me go."

"You've been ruining everything we've thought up all summer," Dudley said, "and you're not setting foot inside this pasture."

In the end they dragged me back to the house, and I ran screaming into the kitchen where Grannie and Calvin, the black man who did the cooking, tried to comfort me, feeding me pound cake and offering to let me help with the mayonnaise.

"You be a sweet girl, Rhoda," my grandmother said, "and this afternoon we'll go over to Eisenglas Plantation to play with Miss Ann Wentzel."

"I don't want to play with Miss Ann Wentzel," I screamed. "I hate Miss Ann Wentzel. She's fat and she calls me a Yankee. She said my socks were ugly."

"Why, Rhoda," my grandmother said. "I'm surprised at you. Miss Ann Wentzel is your own sweet friend. Her momma was your momma's roommate at All Saint's. How can you talk like that?"

"She's a nigger," I screamed. "She's a goddamned nigger German spy."

"Now it's coming. Here comes the temper," Calvin said, rolling his eyes back in their sockets to make me madder. I threw my second fit of the morning, beating my fists into a door frame. My grandmother seized me in soft arms. She led me to a bedroom where I sobbed myself to sleep in a sea of down pillows.

The construction went on for several weeks. As soon as they finished breakfast every morning they started out for the pasture. Wood had to be burned to make cinders, sawdust brought from the sawmill, sand hauled up from the riverbank by wheelbarrow.

When the pit was finished the savage training began. From my several vantage points I watched them. Up and down, up and down they ran, dove, flew, sprinted. Drenched with sweat they wrestled each other to the ground in bitter feuds over distances and times and fractions of inches.

Dudley was their self-appointed leader. He drove them like a demon. They began each morning by running around the edge of the pasture several times, then practicing their hurdles and dashes, then on to discus throwing and calisthenics. Then on to the Broad Jump Pit with its endless challenges.

They even pressed the old mare into service. Saint John was from New Orleans and knew the British ambassador and was thinking of being a polo player. Up and down the pasture he drove the poor old creature, leaning far out of the saddle, swatting a basketball with my grandaddy's cane.

I spied on them from the swing that went out over the bayou, and from the roof of the chicken house, and sometimes from the pasture fence itself, calling out insults or attempts to make them jealous.

"Guess what," I would yell, "I'm going to town to the Chinaman's store." "Guess what, I'm getting to go to the beauty parlor." "Doctor Biggs says you're adopted."

They ignored me. At meals they sat together at one end of the table, making jokes about my temper and my red hair, opening their mouths so I could see their half-chewed food, burping loudly in my direction.

At night they pulled their cots together on the sleeping porch, plotting against me while I slept beneath my grandmother's window, listening to the soft assurance of her snoring.

I began to pray the Japs would win the war, would come marching into Issaquena County and take them prisoners, starving and torturing them, sticking bamboo splinters under their fingernails. I saw myself in the Japanese colonel's office, turning them in, writing their names down, myself being treated like an honored guest, drinking tea from tiny blue cups like the ones the Chinaman had in his store.

They would be outside, tied up with wire. There would be Dudley, begging for mercy. What good to him now his loyal gang, his photographic memory, his trick magnet dogs, his perfect pitch, his camp shorts, his Baby Brownie camera.

I prayed they would get polio, would be consigned forever to iron lungs. I put myself to sleep at night imagining their labored breathing, their five little wheelchairs lined up by the store as I drove by in my father's Packard, my arm around the jacket of his blue uniform, on my way to Hollywood for my screen test.

Meanwhile, I practiced dancing. My grandmother had a black housekeeper named Baby Doll who was a wonderful dancer. In the mornings I followed her around while she dusted, begging for dancing lessons. She was a big woman, as tall as a man, and gave off a dark rich smell, an unforgettable incense, a combination of Evening in Paris and the sweet perfume of the cabins.

Baby Doll wore bright skirts and on her blouses a pin that said REMEMBER, then a real pearl, then HARBOR. She was engaged to a sailor and was going to California to be rich as soon as the war was over.

I would put a stack of heavy, scratched records on the record player, and Baby Doll and I would dance through the parlors to the music of Glenn Miller or Guy Lombardo or Tommy Dorsey.

Sometimes I stood on a stool in front of the fireplace and made up lyrics while Baby Doll acted them out, moving lightly across the old dark rugs, turning and swooping and shaking and gliding.

Outside the summer sun beat down on the Delta, beating down a million volts a minute, feeding the soybeans and cotton and clover, sucking Steele's Bayou up into the clouds, beating down on the road and the store, on the pecans and elms and magnolias, on the men at work in the fields, on the athletes at work in the pasture.

Inside Baby Doll and I would be dancing. Or Guy Lombardo would be playing "Begin the Beguine" and I would be belting out lyrics.

> *"Oh, let them begin . . . we don't care,*
> *America all . . . ways does its share,*
> *We'll be there with plenty of ammo,*
> *Allies . . . don't ever despair . . ."*

Baby Doll thought I was a genius. If I was having an especially creative morning she would go running out to the kitchen and bring anyone she could find to hear me.

"Oh, let them begin any warrr . . ." I would be singing, tapping one foot against the fireplace tiles, waving my arms around like a conductor.

> *"Uncle Sam will fight*
> *for the underrr . . . doggg.*
> *Never fear, Allies, never fear."*

A new record would drop. Baby Doll would swoop me into her fragrant arms, and we would break into an improvisation on Tommy Dorsey's "Boogie-Woogie."

But the Broad Jump Pit would not go away. It loomed in my dreams. If I walked to the store I had to pass the pasture. If I stood on the porch or looked out my grandmother's window, there it was, shimmering in the sunlight, constantly guarded by one of the Olympians.

Things went from bad to worse between me and Dudley. If we so much as passed each other in the hall a fight began. He would hold up his fists and dance around, trying to look like a fighter. When I came flailing at him he would reach underneath my arms and punch me in the stomach.

I considered poisoning him. There was a box of white powder in the toolshed with a skull and crossbones above the label. Several times I took it down and held it in my hands, shuddering at the power it gave me. Only the thought of the electric chair kept me from using it.

Every day Dudley gathered his troops and headed out for the pasture. Every day my hatred grew and festered. Then, just about the time I could stand it no longer, a diversion occurred.

One afternoon about four o'clock an official-looking sedan

clattered across the bridge and came roaring down the road to the house.

It was my cousin, Lauralee Manning, wearing her WAVE uniform and smoking Camels in an ivory holder. Lauralee had been widowed at the beginning of the war when her young husband crashed his Navy training plane into the Pacific.

Lauralee dried her tears, joined the WAVES, and went off to avenge his death. I had not seen this paragon since I was a small child, but I had memorized the photograph Miss Onnie Maud, who was Lauralee's mother, kept on her dresser. It was a photograph of Lauralee leaning against the rail of a destroyer.

Not that Lauralee ever went to sea on a destroyer. She was spending the war in Pensacola, Florida, being secretary to an admiral.

Now, out of a clear blue sky, here was Lauralee, home on leave with a two-carat diamond ring and the news that she was getting married.

"You might have called and given some warning," Miss Onnie Maud said, turning Lauralee into a mass of wrinkles with her embraces. "You could have softened the blow with a letter."

"Who's the groom," my grandmother said. "I only hope he's not a pilot."

"Is he an admiral?" I said, "or a colonel or a major or a commander?"

"My fiancé's not in uniform, Honey," Lauralee said. "He's in real estate. He runs the war-bond effort for the whole state of Florida. Last year he collected half a million dollars."

"In real estate!" Miss Onnie Maud said, gasping. "What religion is he?"

"He's Unitarian," she said. "His name is Donald Marcus. He's best friends with Admiral Semmes, that's how I met him. And he's coming a week from Saturday, and that's all the time we have to get ready for the wedding."

"Unitarian!" Miss Onnie Maud said. "I don't think I've ever met a Unitarian."

"Why isn't he in uniform?" I insisted.

"He has flat feet," Lauralee said gaily. "But you'll love him when you see him."

117

Later that afternoon Lauralee took me off by myself for a ride in the sedan.

"Your mother is my favorite cousin," she said, touching my face with gentle fingers. "You'll look just like her when you grow up and get your figure."

I moved closer, admiring the brass buttons on her starched uniform and the brisk way she shifted and braked and put in the clutch and accelerated.

We drove down the river road and out to the bootlegger's shack where Lauralee bought a pint of Jack Daniel's and two Cokes. She poured out half of her Coke, filled it with whiskey, and we roared off down the road with the radio playing.

We drove along in the lengthening day. Lauralee was chain-smoking, lighting one Camel after another, tossing the butts out the window, taking sips from her bourbon and Coke. I sat beside her, pretending to smoke a piece of rolled-up paper, making little noises into the mouth of my Coke bottle.

We drove up to a picnic spot on the levee and sat under a tree to look out at the river.

"I miss this old river," she said. "When I'm sad I dream about it licking the tops of the levees."

I didn't know what to say to that. To tell the truth I was afraid to say much of anything to Lauralee. She seemed so splendid. It was enough to be allowed to sit by her on the levee.

"Now, Rhoda," she said, "your mother was matron of honor in my wedding to Buddy, and I want you, her own little daughter, to be maid of honor in my second wedding."

I could hardly believe my ears! While I was trying to think of something to say to this wonderful news I saw that Lauralee was crying, great tears were forming in her blue eyes.

"Under this very tree is where Buddy and I got engaged," she said. Now the tears were really starting to roll, falling all over the front of her uniform. "He gave me my ring right where we're sitting."

"The maid of honor?" I said, patting her on the shoulder, trying to be of some comfort. "You really mean the maid of honor?"

"Now he's gone from the world," she continued, "and I'm

marrying a wonderful man, but that doesn't make it any easier. Oh, Rhoda, they never even found his body, never even found his body."

I was patting her on the head now, afraid she would forget her offer in the midst of her sorrow.

"You mean I get to be the real maid of honor?"

"Oh, yes, Rhoda, Honey," she said. "The maid of honor, my only attendant." She blew her nose on a lace-trimmed handkerchief and sat up straighter, taking a drink from the Coke bottle.

"Not only that, but I have decided to let you pick out your own dress. We'll go to Greenville and you can try on every dress at Nell's and Blum's and you can have the one you like the most."

I threw my arms around her, burning with happiness, smelling her whiskey and Camels and the dark Tabu perfume that was her signature. Over her shoulder and through the low branches of the trees the afternoon sun was going down in an orgy of reds and blues and purples and violets, falling from sight, going all the way to China.

Let them keep their nasty Broad Jump Pit I thought. Wait till they hear about this. Wait till they find out I'm maid of honor in a military wedding.

Finding the dress was another matter. Early the next morning Miss Onnie Maud and my grandmother and Lauralee and I set out for Greenville.

As we passed the pasture I hung out the back window making faces at the athletes. This time they only pretended to ignore me. They couldn't ignore this wedding. It was going to be in the parlor instead of the church so they wouldn't even get to be altar boys. They wouldn't get to light a candle.

"I don't know why you care what's going on in that pasture," my grandmother said. "Even if they let you play with them all it would do is make you a lot of ugly muscles."

"Then you'd have big old ugly arms like Weegie Toler," Miss Onnie Maud said. "Lauralee, you remember Weegie Toler, that was a swimmer. Her arms got so big no one would take her to a dance, much less marry her."

"Well, I don't want to get married anyway," I said. "I'm

never getting married. I'm going to New York City and be a lawyer."

"Where does she get those ideas?" Miss Onnie Maud said.

"When you get older you'll want to get married," Lauralee said. "Look at how much fun you're having being in my wedding."

"Well, I'm never getting married," I said. "And I'm never having any children. I'm going to New York and be a lawyer and save people from the electric chair."

"It's the movies," Miss Onnie Maud said. "They let her watch anything she likes in Indiana."

We walked into Nell's and Blum's Department Store and took up the largest dressing room. My grandmother and Miss Onnie Maud were seated on brocade chairs and every saleslady in the store came crowding around trying to get in on the wedding.

I refused to even consider the dresses they brought from the "girls'" department.

"I told her she could wear whatever she wanted," Lauralee said, "and I'm keeping my promise."

"Well, she's not wearing green satin or I'm not coming," my grandmother said, indicating the dress I had found on a rack and was clutching against me.

"At least let her try in on," Lauralee said. "Let her see for herself." She zipped me into the green satin. It came down to my ankles and fit around my midsection like a girdle, making my waist seem smaller than my stomach. I admired myself in the mirror. It was almost perfect. I looked exactly like a nightclub singer.

"This one's fine," I said. "This is the one I want."

"It looks marvelous, Rhoda," Lauralee said, "but it's the wrong color for the wedding. Remember I'm wearing blue."

"I believe the child's color-blind," Miss Onnie Maud said. "It runs in her father's family."

"I am not color-blind," I said, reaching behind me and unzipping the dress. "I have twenty-twenty vision."

"Let her try on some more," Lauralee said. "Let her try on everything in the store."

I proceeded to do just that, with the salesladies getting grumpier and grumpier. I tried on a gold gabardine dress with a rhinestone-studded cumberbund. I tried on a pink ballerina-length formal and a lavender voile tea dress and several silk suits. Somehow nothing looked right.

"Maybe we'll have to make her something," my grandmother said.

"But there's no time," Miss Onnie Maud said. "Besides first we'd have to find out what she wants. Rhoda, please tell us what you're looking for."

Their faces all turned to mine, waiting for an answer. But I didn't know the answer.

The dress I wanted was a secret. The dress I wanted was dark and tall and thin as a reed. There was a word for what I wanted, a word I had seen in magazines. But what was that word? I could not remember.

"I want something dark," I said at last. "Something dark and silky."

"Wait right there," the saleslady said. "Wait just a minute." Then, from out of a prewar storage closet she brought a black-watch plaid recital dress with spaghetti straps and a white piqué jacket. It was made of taffeta and rustled when I touched it. There was a label sewn into the collar of the jacket. *Little Miss Sophisticate*, it said. *Sophisticate*, that was the word I was seeking.

I put on the dress and stood triumphant in a sea of ladies and dresses and hangers.

"This is the dress," I said. "This is the dress I'm wearing."

"It's perfect," Lauralee said. "Start hemming it up. She'll be the prettiest maid of honor in the whole world."

All the way home I held the box on my lap thinking about how I would look in the dress. Wait till they see me like this, I was thinking. Wait till they see what I really look like.

I fell in love with the groom. The moment I laid eyes on him I forgot he was flat-footed. He arrived bearing gifts of music and perfume and candy, a warm dark-skinned man with eyes the color of walnuts.

He laughed out loud when he saw me, standing on the porch with my hands on my hips.

"This must be Rhoda," he exclaimed, "the famous red-haired maid of honor." He came running up the steps, gave me a slow, exciting hug, and presented me with a whole album of Xavier Cugat records. I had never owned a record of my own, much less an album.

Before the evening was over I put on a red formal I found in a trunk and did a South American dance for him to Xavier Cugat's "Poinciana." He said he had never seen anything like it in his whole life.

The wedding itself was a disappointment. No one came but the immediate family and there was no aisle to march down and the only music was Onnie Maud playing "Liebestraum."

Dudley and Philip and Saint John and Oliver and Bunky were dressed in long pants and white shirts and ties. They had fresh military crew cuts and looked like a nest of new birds, huddled together on the blue velvet sofa, trying to keep their hands to themselves, trying to figure out how to act at a wedding.

The elderly Episcopal priest read out the ceremony in a gravelly smoker's voice, ruining all the good parts by coughing. He was in a bad mood because Lauralee and Mr. Marcus hadn't found time to come to him for marriage instruction.

Still, I got to hold the bride's flowers while he gave her the ring and stood so close to her during the ceremony I could hear her breathing.

The reception was better. People came from all over the Delta. There were tables with candles set up around the porches and sprays of greenery in every corner. There were gentlemen sweating in linen suits and the record player playing every minute. In the back hall Calvin had set up a real professional bar with tall, permanently frosted glasses and ice and mint and lemons and every kind of whiskey and liqueur in the world.

I stood in the receiving line getting compliments on my dress, then wandered around the rooms eating cake and letting people hug me. After a while I got bored with that and went out to the back hall and began to fix myself a drink at the bar.

I took one of the frosted glasses and began filling it from different bottles, tasting as I went along. I used plenty of crème de menthe and soon had something that tasted heavenly. I filled the glass with crushed ice, added three straws, and went out to sit on the back steps and cool off.

I was feeling wonderful. A full moon was caught like a kite in the pecan trees across the river. I sipped along on my drink. Then, without planning it, I did something I had never dreamed of doing. I left the porch alone at night. Usually I was in terror of the dark. My grandmother had told me that alligators come out of the bayou to eat children who wander alone at night.

I walked out across the yard, the huge moon giving so much light I almost cast a shadow. When I was nearly to the water's edge I turned and looked back toward the house. It shimmered in the moonlight like a jukebox alive in a meadow, seemed to pulsate with music and laughter and people, beautiful and foreign, not a part of me.

I looked out at the water, then down the road to the pasture. The Broad Jump Pit! There it was, perfect and unguarded. Why had I never thought of doing this before?

I began to run toward the road. I ran as fast as my Mary Jane pumps would allow me. I pulled my dress up around my waist and climbed the fence in one motion, dropping lightly down on the other side. I was sweating heavily, alone with the moon and my wonderful courage.

I knew exactly what to do first. I picked up the pole and hoisted it over my head. It felt solid and balanced and alive. I hoisted it up and down a few times as I had seen Dudley do, getting the feel of it.

Then I laid it ceremoniously down on the ground, reached behind me, and unhooked the plaid formal. I left it lying in a heap on the ground. There I stood, in my cotton underpants, ready to take up pole-vaulting.

I lifted the pole and carried it back to the end of the cinder path. I ran slowly down the path, stuck the pole in the wooden cup, and attempted throwing my body into the air, using it as a lever.

Something was wrong. It was more difficult than it appeared from a distance. I tried again. Nothing happened. I sat down with the pole across my legs to think things over.

Then I remembered something I had watched Dudley

doing through the binoculars. He measured down from the end of the pole with his fingers spread wide. That was it, I had to hold it closer to the end.

I tried it again. This time the pole lifted me several feet off the ground. My body sailed across the grass in a neat arc and I landed on my toes. I was a natural!

I do not know how long I was out there, running up and down the cinder path, thrusting my body further and further through space, tossing myself into the pit like a mussel shell thrown across the bayou.

At last I decided I was ready for the real test. I had to vault over a cane barrier. I examined the pegs on the wooden poles and chose one that came up to my shoulder.

I put the barrier pole in place, spit over my left shoulder, and marched back to the end of the path. Suck up your guts, I told myself. It's only a pole. It won't get stuck in your stomach and tear out your insides. It won't kill you.

I stood at the end of the path eyeballing the barrier. Then, above the incessant racket of the crickets, I heard my name being called. Rhoda . . . the voices were calling. Rhoda . . . Rhoda . . . Rhoda . . . Rhoda.

I turned toward the house and saw them coming. Mr. Marcus and Dudley and Bunky and Calvin and Lauralee and what looked like half the wedding. They were climbing the fence, calling my name, and coming to get me. Rhoda . . . they called out. Where on earth have you been? What on earth are you doing?

I hoisted the pole up to my shoulders and began to run down the path, running into the light from the moon. I picked up speed, thrust the pole into the cup, and threw myself into the sky, into the still Delta night. I sailed up and was clear and over the barrier.

I let go of the pole and began my fall, which seemed to last a long, long time. It was like falling through clear water. I dropped into the sawdust and lay very still, waiting for them to reach me.

Sometimes I think whatever has happened since has been of no real interest to me.

1944

When I was eight years old I had a piano made of nine martini glasses.

I could have had a real piano if I had been able to pay the terrible price, been able to put up with piano lessons, but the old German spy who taught piano in the small town of Seymour, Indiana, was jealous of my talent.

"Stop it! Stop it! Stop it!" she would scream in her guttural accent, hitting me on the knuckles with the stick she kept for that purpose. "Stopping this crazy business. Can't you ever listen? Can't you sit still a minute? Can't you settle down?"

God knows I tried to settle down. But the mere sight of the magnificent black upright, the feel of the piano stool against my plump bottom, the cold ivory touch of the keys would send me into paroxysms of musical bliss, and I would throw back my head and begin to pound out melodies in two octaves.

"Stop it," she would be screaming. "This is no music, this crazy banging business. Stop on my piano. Stop before I call your momma!"

I remember the day I quit for good. I got up from the piano stool, slammed the cover down on the keys, told her my father would have her arrested, and stalked out of the house without my hat and gloves. It was a cold November day, and I walked home with gray skies all around me, shivering and brokenhearted, certain the secret lives of musical instruments were closed to me forever.

So music might have disappeared from my life. With my formal training at this sorry end I might have had to content myself with tap and ballet and public speaking, but a muse looked down from heaven and took pity on me.

She arrived in the form of a glamorous war widow, was waiting for me at the bar when I walked into the officers' club with my parents that Saturday night.

There she sat, wearing black taffeta, smoking long white cigarettes, sipping her third very dry martini.

"Isn't that Doris Treadway at the bar?" my mother said. "I can't believe she's going out in public."

"What would you like her to do," my father said, "stay home and go crazy?"

"Well, after all," my mother whispered. "It's only been a month."

"Do you *know* that lady?" I asked, wondering if she was a movie star. She looked exactly like a movie star.

"She works for your daddy, Honey," my mother said. "Her husband got killed in the Philippines."

"Go talk to her," my father said. "Go cheer her up. Go tell her who you are."

As soon as we ordered dinner I did just that. I walked across the room and took up the stool beside her at the bar. I breathed deeply of her cool perfume, listening to the rustling of her sleeves as she took a long sophisticated drag on her Camel.

"So you are Dudley's daughter," she said, smiling at me. I squirmed with delight beneath her approving gaze, enchanted by the dark timbre of her voice, the marvelous fuchsia of her lips and fingertips, the brooding glamor of her widowhood.

"I'm Rhoda," I said. "The baby-sitter quit so they brought me with them."

"Would you like a drink?" she asked. "Could I persuade you to join me?"

"Sure," I said. "Sure I'll join you."

She conferred with the bartender and waved to my parents who were watching us from across the room.

"Well, Rhoda," she said. "I've been hearing about you from your father."

"What did you hear?" I asked, getting worried.

"Well," she said, "the best thing I heard was that you locked yourself in a bathroom for six hours to keep from eating fruit cocktail."

"I hate fruit cocktail," I said. "It makes me sick. I wouldn't eat fruit cocktail for all the tea in China."

"I couldn't agree with you more," she said, picking up her stirrer and tapping it on her martini glass. "I think people who hate fruit cocktail should always stick together."

The stirrer made a lovely sound against the glass. The bartender returned, bringing a wineglass full of bright pink liquid.

"Taste it," she said, "go ahead. He made it just for you."

I picked up the glass in two fingers and brought it delicately to my lips as I had seen her do.

"It's wonderful," I said, "what's in it?"

"Something special," she said. "It's called a Shirley Temple. So little girls can pretend they're drinking." She laughed out loud and began to tap the glass stirrer against the line of empty glasses in front of her.

"Why doesn't he move the empty glasses?" I asked.

"Because I'm playing them," she said. "Listen." She tapped out a little tune. "Now, listen to this," she said, adding small amounts of water to the glasses. She tapped them again with the stirrer, calling out the notes in a very high, very clear soprano voice. "Do, Re, Mi, Fa, So, . . . Bartender," she called, "bring us more glasses."

In a minute she had arranged a keyboard with nine perfect notes.

"Here," she said, moving the glasses in front of me, handing me the stirrer, "you play it."

"What should I play," I said. "I don't know any music."

"Of course you know music," she said. "Everyone knows music. Play anything you like. Play whatever comes into your head."

I began to hit the glasses with the stirrer, gingerly at first, then with more abandon. Soon I had something going that sounded marvelous.

"Is that by any chance the 'Air Corps Hymn' you're playing?" she said.

"Well . . . yes it is," I said. "How could you tell?"

She began to sing along with me, singing the words in her perfect voice as I beat upon the glasses. "Off we go," she sang, "into the wild blue yonder, climbing high into the sky, dum, dum, dum. Down we dive spouting a flame from under, off with one hell-of-a-roar, roar, roar . . ."

People crowded around our end of the bar, listening to us, applauding. We finished with the air corps and started right in on the army. "Over hill, over dale, as we hit the dusty trail, and those caissons go marching along, dum, dum, dum . . . In and out, hear them shout, counter march and right about, and those caissons go rolling along. For it's hie, hie, hee, in the field artilll-a-reeeee . . ."

A man near me began playing the bass on a brandy glass. Another man drummed on the bar with a pair of ashtrays.

Doris broke into "Begin the Beguine." "When they begin the beguine," she sang, "it brings back a night of tropical splendor. It brings back the sound of music so te-en-de-rr. It brings back a memorreeeeee ever green."

A woman in a green dress began dancing, swaying to our rhythm. My martini glasses shone in the light from the bar. As I struck them one by one the notes floated around me like bright translucent boats.

This was music! Not the stale order of the book and the metronome, not the stick and the German. Music was this wildness rising from the dark taffeta of Doris's dress. This praise, this brilliance.

The soft delicious light, the smell of perfume and gin, the perfection of our artistry almost overwhelmed me, but I played bravely on.

Every now and then I would look up and see Doris smiling at me while she sang. Doris and I were one. And that too was the secret of music.

I do not know how long we played. Perhaps we played until my dinner was served. Perhaps we played for hours. Perhaps we are playing still.

"Oh, just let them begin the beguine, let them plaaaaay . . . Let the fire that was once a flame remain an ember. Let it burn like the long lost desire I only remember. When they begin, when they begin, when they begi-i-i-i-in the begui-i-i-ine . . ."

Perils of the Nile

Rhoda got up from her seat just as the house lights were going on, licked the rest of the Milky Way from her fingers, and looked around to see if any of the boys she liked were still there. Bebber Dyson was half-asleep in his usual Saturday afternoon seat, but he was too small and dark and poor to be of any real interest to Rhoda, even if he had shown her the eight-page book when they were collecting paper for the sixth-grade paper drive.

She rubbed her tongue across her teeth and gave a little shudder thinking of the picture of Dick Tracy sticking his thing into the dog.

She waved at Bebber and he started her way. Well, he was better than no one at all she thought. After all, he was the best basketball player in the whole school. He was such a good basketball player the seventh grade let him play in their games.

It was a mystery to Rhoda that Bebber was such a good basketball player. No one knew where he came from. He didn't have a proper home. He didn't have regular meals or ironed clothes or parents that went to the PTA. All he had was a father that drank and some rooms above a store.

It belied everything Rhoda knew about basketball. Rhoda's brother had special basketball shoes and special pre-game basketball training meals and his own basketball goal above the garage door to practice on. Rhoda's father even had the concrete people come and pour concrete under the goal so they could mark off the free throw lines.

But no matter how many hours Rhoda's brother stood at the free throw line practicing shots he could only get the ball through the hoop half the time.

Bebber Dyson's shots always went through the hoop. He could shoot sideways and underhanded and over his head and one-handed and two-handed and every single time the basketball went through the hoop. Perhaps it was because he stayed at the pool hall all the time Rhoda thought. Perhaps it was because he was poor. Maybe you have to be poor to be a good basketball player.

"How you doing?" Bebber said, coming up beside her, smiling his wide smile. His teeth were very white and even like a movie star's. He was wearing his blue polo shirt. He wore the same shirt nearly every day, but he was always clean and he smelled nice. He didn't smell bad like most poor people.

"Where's your friend, Cynthia?" he asked. "She didn't come with you today?"

"She had to go riding with her mother," Rhoda said. "They made her go. She almost died she wanted to see this picture so much. Gene Kelly's her favorite. She loves him."

Cynthia was Rhoda's best friend. Her mother was always taking her off horseback riding on the weekends. It made Rhoda's heart burn with envy and admiration to see them going off in their boots and jodhpurs. Rhoda wondered if Bebber was in love with Cynthia. Cynthia had funny taste in boys. Come to think of it Bebber did look something like Gene Kelly.

"I don't like Gene Kelly very much myself," she said. "I think he looks kind of like a girl."

"He's a good dancer," Bebber said.

"He's O.K.," Rhoda said, "but he smiles too much."

"Where you going now?" Bebber asked. "You want to go to the drugstore and see if anyone's there?"

"Sure," Rhoda said. She wasn't sure if it was a good idea to be seen with Bebber, but she liked the idea of going in the drugstore with a boy. Maybe someone would think they had a date. Maybe Joe Franke would see her and think Bebber loved her.

"Hey," she said. "You want to see what I got today. Look at this." She held out her hand. Then she froze, looking down at her hand in horror. It was gone.

The ring was gone. Her brand-new antique pearl ring that had come in the mail from her grandmother that very morning was gone. She stared down at her finger, cold and disbelieving. It was not there. Her grandmother's own pearl ring that had come in the mail from Mississippi, her long-awaited birthday ring, her heirloom, her precious heirloom pearl solitaire ring that she was not under any circumstances supposed to wear was no longer on her finger.

"Bebber," she said. "Bebber, I've lost my ring." She dropped to the floor on her knees and began searching under the seats with her fingers, running her hands through the sticky jumble of popcorn sacks and candy wrappers and Coca-Cola cups.

"What does it look like?" he said, kneeling beside her, blocking the aisle where the last stragglers from the Saturday matinee were making their way out into the sunlit world of Seymour, Indiana.

"It's a pearl," she said. "It's a real pearl solitaire set in gold. It's valuable. It's worth about a hundred dollars and my grandmother sent it for my birthday and they're going to kill me for losing it."

"Well, calm down," Bebber said. "We'll find it. Just calm down and pick up everything that's down there and shake it out." He dropped to his knees beside her, smelling the sweet sweaty smell of her blouse. She was a strange girl, a funny girl who talked all the time and acted like she wasn't afraid of anything, not even the teacher. Once she faked a faint on the playground and was taken home in the principal's car without once opening her eyes or admitting she could hear.

He had walked her home one afternoon after school, and her mother made chocolate milk for them and stayed in the kitchen talking to them while they drank it. She praised him when he picked up his glass and rinsed it in the sink.

Bebber thought about Rhoda's mother a lot. She was very beautiful and had looked straight at him out of sad blue eyes while he talked about himself. Rhoda's whole family were strange people. They had come to Seymour from the south and talked a strange soft way. Whenever he passed their house he wished he could go in and talk to Rhoda's mother some more.

"If I don't find it they're going to kill me," she said. "They're going to murder me."

"Where do you think you lost it?" he asked, running his hand up and down the grooves between the folding seats.

"I don't know," she said, "but I had it when I came in the show because I showed it to Letitia. Letitia said it was the prettiest thing she'd ever seen in her life."

"Maybe it got in your popcorn sack," Bebber said. "Maybe you ate it."

"I did not eat it," Rhoda said. Rhoda was very conscious of her figure. She hated to be reminded that she ever ate anything. "And that isn't funny, Bebber. And if I don't find that ring they're going to kill me."

"I'm sorry," he said. "I'll get the usher. We can use his flashlight. You be picking up the rest of the paper." As Bebber started to rise up from the floor he felt the ring, cold and flat beneath his fingers on the worn runner of the aisle carpet. His fingers closed around it and he stood up and stuck his hands into his pockets.

"I'll be back," he said. "You keep on looking."

He returned with the usher, and the three of them searched the floor and seats for a long time, retracing Rhoda's steps from the time she came into the theater, shaking out every piece of paper and box and cup and poking down into dozens of seats and crannies.

"Maybe you didn't really have it on," Bebber said. "Maybe you just thought you wore it."

"I had it," Rhoda said. "I showed it to Letitia."

"There's no place else to look," the usher said. "And the manager wants to close up now. We're having a special show tonight for the war effort. Everyone that brings a piece of steel gets in free. It's *Journey for Margaret* with Margaret O'Brien."

"But what about my ring?" Rhoda said. "How'll I ever find it?"

"We'll make an announcement tonight," the usher said. "How about that. We'll announce that anyone that finds it should turn it in to the box office."

"All right," Rhoda said. "I guess that's all I can do."

"Come on," Bebber said. "Let's go over to the drugstore and see if anyone's there."

"I don't feel like it now." Rhoda said. "I better go on home."

"You want me to go home with you?" Bebber asked. "You want me to help you tell your mother?"

"No," she said. "I probably won't tell her until I have to. She's going to murder me when she finds out."

When Rhoda got home she went up to her room, closed the door, and threw herself down on the eiderdown comforter. Why does everything have to happen to me she thought. *Every time something happens it happens to me.* She rubbed her face deep down into the silk comforter, feeling the cool fabric against her cheeks, smelling the queer dead odor of the down feathers. She pulled out a few pieces where the little white tips were working their way out of the silk.

The eiderdown comforter was Rhoda's favorite thing in the house. It was dark red on one side and pink on the other. Rhoda liked to roll up in it on hot afternoons and pretend she was Cleopatra waiting for Mark Antony to come kiss her.

Sometimes Cynthia would play the game with her, but Cynthia made a desultory Roman general and her kisses were brief and cold and absentminded. It was better to play Cleopatra alone.

When she was alone Rhoda pretended the bed was a barge floating down the Nile and she was the queen reclining on a silken couch being fed by slaves, her hair combed and perfumed, her sleek half-naked body being pampered and touched and adored a thousand ways. She lay still, quiet and gracious, watching the shore glide by as she surveyed her kingdom.

Rhoda's bed was a cherry four-poster, and she could lie on her stomach on top of the comforter and rock the mattress back and forth by the pressure of her feet against the footboard. She would rock like that until she fell asleep, feeling strange and lost in time, a dark queen full of languorous passions.

Today, however, the quilt was of no comfort to her. She was not due to have another valuable ring until her mother died and left her a diamond and that might be a long time as women in her family lived to ripe old ages.

It occurred to her that she might pray for the ring. Usually Rhoda wasn't much on praying. When she said her prayers at night all she thought about was Jesus coming to get her in a chariot filled with angels. She didn't want Jesus to come get her. She didn't want to be lying in a box like Jerry Hollister, who was run over in his driveway by his own brother home on leave from the air corps.

The whole fifth grade had gone to see Jerry lying in his casket. His face was white as chalk and he was wearing a suit, lying on his dining room table in a casket with his eyes permanently closed.

Rhoda didn't want anything to do with that. She didn't want anything to do with Jesus or religion or little boys lying on their dining room tables with their eyes closed.

When they made Rhoda go to church on Sundays she pretended she was someplace else. She didn't want anything to do with God and Jesus and dead people and people nailed up on crosses or eaten by lions or tortured by Romans.

This matter of the ring, however, was an emergency. At any moment Rhoda's mother might call up the stairs and ask her to bring the ring to show to someone.

I could pretend it was stolen she thought. I could say Del Rio stole it. Del Rio was the black woman who lived with them. Del Rio had come on a bus from Mississippi when Rhoda's baby brother was born. Rhoda hated Del Rio. Del Rio was always lecturing Rhoda about not drinking out of the water bottle and threatening to sic a big dog on her if she didn't stop teasing the baby. It would serve Del Rio right to go to jail for stealing.

Of course it would never work. Del Rio would kill her, would come for her with a knife. Besides, the man at the picture show was going to announce that she had lost it. Everyone in town would be calling up to see if they had found it.

I might as well pray, Rhoda said, getting up off the bed and looking around the room for a nice place to do some praying. The closet, Rhoda thought. That's the best place. She went into the closet and pulled the door shut behind her. Her dresses and blouses hung primly on their pink silk hangers. Her shoe bags hung on the door beside her bowed head.

"Well, Jesus," Rhoda said, beginning her prayer. "You know I have to get that ring back. So if you will get it back to me I promise I'll start believing in you." She waited a minute to let that sink in, then continued.

"If you'll help me find it I'll be nice to everyone from now

134

on. I won't yell at anyone and I won't stick my finger in my crack when I take a bath. I'll quit lying so much. I'll quit hating Dudley and I'll quit giving Cokes to the baby. If you'll help me find it I'll do everything you want from now on. I'll even go overseas and be a missionary if that's what you want."

Rhoda liked that idea. She could see herself standing on a distant seashore handing out bright fabrics to the childlike natives. Rhoda was beginning to feel quite holy. She was beginning to like talking to Jesus.

"Jesus," she continued, squirming around on the floor to get in a more prayerful position, picturing Jesus on a hill surrounded by his sheep. "Jesus," she said, "to tell the truth I have always believed in you. And I'll be going to Sunday school all the time now if I get my ring back."

It was very quiet in the closet. Rhoda could feel Jesus thinking. She felt him lay his hand upon her head. Jesus said he would think it over.

Rhoda got up from her knees in a reverent manner and left the closet with her hands still folded. She was feeling better. The oppression that had weighed her down all afternoon was lifting. It was up to Jesus now. She decided to go downstairs and shoot some baskets with Dudley until time for supper.

Bebber Dyson sat down on the unmade bed, took the ring from his pocket, and examined it in the light coming in on a slant through the low windows. His face was very still, and the high Indian cheekbones of his grandfather cast long shadows along the ridge of his nose.

Bebber studied his treasure. It was an old-fashioned solitaire, a small pearl set in five slender prongs of gold.

He touched the top of the pearl with his finger, then put it on and held his hand away from him, imagining Rhoda's mother's slender white hands.

The ring was like her, elegant and still and foreign. Someday, he thought, he would drive a big car down a street to a house where a woman like that waited. Everything around her would be quiet and clean and she would hand him something to drink in a glass.

He wrapped the ring in a piece of tissue paper and returned it to his pocket.

Then he got up and made the bed, folding the corners neatly and smoothing out all the wrinkles.

Next he walked around the small apartment, emptying the ashtrays and wiping off the flat surfaces with a towel. He swept the floor, picked up the sweepings in a dustpan, and deposited them in a paper sack.

He removed his clothes and laid them on the bed to inspect them for spots. He walked over to the sink and carefully washed out the blue shirt, scrubbing it good with plenty of soap, rinsing it and hanging it on a hanger by the window.

Then he began to wash himself, very carefully and thoroughly, beginning with his hair, working down to his arms and chest and legs and feet. He washed himself as if he were some foreign object, oblivious to the beauty and symmetry of his body, to the smooth shine of his olive skin, to the order and intelligence of his parts.

He dried himself, then wiped up the mess the water had made on the floor. He brushed and parted his hair and dressed carefully in his good clothes, gray pants, white shirt, and a sleeveless dark green sweater.

He walked down the stairs and out onto the street. The early autumn dusk was magical, long rays of red slanting light catching the bottom branches of the elm trees.

He walked down Pershing Avenue to where it turns onto Calvin Boulevard, imagining what Rhoda's mother would be doing this time of day, holding her baby, laughing into his tiny face, walking around her kitchen fixing dinner, her high-heeled shoes clicking on the linoleum.

Maybe she would ask him to stay for chocolate milk. Maybe she would ask him to stay for dinner.

The light was changing now, deepening. Bebber began to hum a little tune to himself as he walked along, feeling clean and lucky, fondling the little package in his pocket, picturing the way her hair moved around her shoulders when she talked.

I will be riding up on a white horse he thought. I will be wearing a uniform and she will be standing on the porch holding her baby. It is too cold for her to be outside like that. I will give her my coat. I will put her on the horse and take her wherever she needs to go. I will walk slowly because it is dangerous to ride that way carrying a baby.

136

Bebber walked on down the street, the rays of the setting sun making him a path all the way to her house, a little road to travel, a wide band of luminous and precarious order.

Traveler

It was June in southern Indiana. I was locked in the upstairs bathroom studying the directions on a box of Tampax when the invitation came.

"LeLe," my father called, coming up the stairs with the letter in his hand. "Come out of there. Come hear the news. You're going to the Delta."

It seems my cousin Baby Gwen Barksdale's mother had died of a weak liver, and rather than leave the poor girl alone in a house with a grieving widower the family had invited me to Mississippi to spend the summer as her companion. There was even a suggestion that I might stay and go to school there in the fall.

What luck that the invitation came just as my own mother, giving in to a fit of jealous rage, left my father and fled to New Orleans to have a nervous breakdown.

"You'll love it in Clarksville," my father assured me. "Baby Gwen is just your age and just your speed. She'll be so glad to see you." And he pressed several more twenty-dollar bills into my hand and helped me pack my summer clothes.

"You try it for the summer, LeLe," he said. "We'll decide about school later on."

He might need to decide later on, but my mind was made up. I couldn't wait to leave Franklin, Indiana, where the students at Franklin Junior High had made the mistake of failing to elect me cheerleader. I wasn't unpopular or anything like that, just a little on the plump side.

Baby Gwen Barksdale, I whispered to myself as I arranged my things on the Pullman seat. I was sweating heavily in a pink linen suit, and my straw hat was making my head itch, but I sat up straight, trying to look like a lady. I had the latest edition of *Hit Parade Magazine* on my lap, and I was determined to learn every word of the Top Ten on the train ride.

Baby Gwen Barksdale, I said to myself, remembering the stories my father had told me. Baby Gwen, queen of the Delta subdeb dances, daughter of the famous Gwendolyn Montgomery Paine of Shaw, granddaughter of my grandmother's sainted sister, Frances Paine of Natchez. Baby Gwen Barksdale, daughter of Britain Barksdale who played halfback on the Ole Miss Sugar Bowl team.

It was all too good to be true. I marched myself down to the diner and ate several desserts to calm myself down.

By the time the Illinois Central made it all the way to Clarksville, Mississippi, my linen dress was helplessly wrinkled, my third pair of white gloves was damp and stained from the dye of the magazine, and my teeth were worn out from being brushed.

But there on the platform she waited, Baby Gwen Barksdale herself, five feet two inches of sultry dark-skinned, dark-eyed beauty. (The Barksdales have French blood.) She looked exactly like Ida Lupino. She was wearing a navy blue dotted Swiss sun dress and high-heeled shoes and her slip was showing, a thin line of ecru lace. Her dark pink lipstick exactly matched her fingernail polish, and she smelled divinely of Aprodisia perfume.

She was accompanied by a strong boy who smiled a lot and turned out to be the sheriff's son. He had come along to carry the luggage.

"I'm so glad you could come," she said, hugging me for the fourth time. "I can't believe you came all the way on the train by yourself."

"No one in Franklin believed I'd do it either," I said. "I just got elected cheerleader and practically the whole football team came to the station to tell me goodbye. They didn't believe I was leaving. Of course, they all know about Bob Aaron. That's the college boy I love. He's got cancer of the thyroid gland. My parents won't let me go out with him because he's Jewish. He's already had about five operations. He's having one right now in St. Louis. So I might as well be down here."

"Oh, LeLe, that's terrible. It's like my mother. I know just how you feel."

"Well, anyway, I'm here now and we can stick together," I said, taking a deep breath of the Aprodisia. "I love your perfume. It's wonderful."

"It's my signature," she said. "I wear Aprodisia in the summer and Tigress in the winter. There's a bottle in my purse. You can put some on if you want to."

We walked over to the Oldsmobile and Baby Gwen got behind the wheel. She was so short she had to sit on straw pillows to see over the dash, but she turned out to be a superb driver. The sheriff's son climbed into the back seat with my bags, and the three of us drove off down the streets of the town, past the gin and the post office and the Pontiac place, and on down the river road to a white frame house at the end of a street that dead-ended at the levee.

So I arrived in Clarksville, chattering away to a spellbound audience, spraying my neck and arms with Aprodisia perfume, happier than I had ever been in my life.

After her mother's funeral Baby Gwen had moved into the master bedroom as her father was too brokenhearted to ever enter that part of the house again.

I was led up the stairs and into a large sunny room with bay windows and a pale blue chaise lounge. There was a dressing room with a private bath and walk-in closets. Everything was just as Big Gwen had left it.

The closets were filled with unbelievable clothes. Navy blue and green and black silk dresses, gray and beige and brown gabardine suits, pastel evening dresses, house dresses, sun dresses, wool coats, skirts, jackets. There were twenty or thirty pairs of high-heeled shoes and a dozen hatboxes. There were drawers full of handmade underwear. There was a fur stole and several negligees and a real Japanese kimono.

It was all ours.

"You can wear anything you want to," Baby Gwen said. "Most of them are too long for me."

Best of all was the dressing table. It was three feet long with a padded stool and a large mirror surrounded by light bulbs.

On its surface, in a sea of spilled powder, were dozens of

bottles and jars. Every product ever manufactured by Charles of the Ritz must have been there. There was foundation cream, astringent, eye shadow, rouge, clarifier, moisturizer, cleanser, refining oil, facial mask, night cream, hand cream, wrinkle cream, eye cream, all pervaded by the unforgettable smell of Revenescence, Charles of the Ritz's secret formula moisturizer.

There were hairpins, hand mirrors, tweezers, eyelash curlers, combs, hair rollers, mascara wands, cuticle sticks, nail polish, emery boards. There were numerous bottles of perfume and cologne and a cut-glass bowl filled with lipsticks.

I had never seen anything like it. I could hardly wait to sit down on the little padded stool and get started.

"You want a Coca-Cola?" Baby Gwen asked, growing bored with my inspection of her riches. "Some boys I know are coming over later this afternoon to meet you."

"Can we smoke?" I asked, pulling my Pall Malls out of my purse.

"We can do anything we want to do," she said, picking a Ronson lighter off the dressing table and handing it to me. She was smiling the famous Barksdale slow smile.

That night we lay awake until two or three in the morning telling each other our life stories. I told her about Bob Aaron's lymph node cancer, and she told me about her cousin Maurice, who taught French and hated Clarksville and was married to an unpleasant woman who sang in the choir. Maurice was secretly in love with Baby Gwen. He couldn't help himself. He had confessed his love at a spring wedding reception. Now they were waiting for Baby Gwen to grow up so they could run away together. In the meantime Baby Gwen was playing the field so no one would suspect.

Finally, exhausted by our passions, we fell asleep in each other's arms, with the night breezes blowing in the windows off the river, in our ironed sheets and our silk pajamas and our night cream, with the radio playing an all-night station from New Orleans. Oh, Bob, Bob, I whispered into Baby Gwen's soft black hair. Oh, Maurice, Maurice, she sighed into my hair rollers.

In the morning I woke early and wandered downstairs. I went into the kitchen, opened the freezer, found a carton of

141

vanilla ice cream, and began to eat it with my fingers, standing with the freezer door open, letting the cool air blow on my face.

After a while I heard the back door slam and Sirena came in. She was the middle-aged black woman who turned out to be the only person in charge of us in any way. Baby Gwen's father disappeared before dawn to carry the mail and came home in the evenings and sank into his chair with his bourbon and his memories. Occasionally he would put in an appearance at the noon meal and ask us if we wanted anything.

I barely managed to close the freezer door before Sirena caught me. "You want me to make you some breakfast?" she said.

"No, thank you," I said. "I don't eat in the daytime. I'm on a diet."

I have always believed Sirena found my fingerprints in that ice cream. One way or the other I wasn't fooling her, she knew a Yankee when she saw one, even if I was Mr. Leland's daughter.

I wandered into the living room and read a *Coronet* for a while Then I decided to go back upstairs and see if Baby Gwen was awake.

I found her in the bathroom sitting upright in a tub of soapy water while Sirena knelt beside it slowly and intently bathing her. I had never seen a grown person being bathed before.

Sirena was running her great black hand up and down Baby Gwen's white leg, soaping her with a terry-cloth washrag. The artesian well water was the color of urine and smelled of sulphur and sandalwood soap, and Sirena's dark hand was thick and strong moving along Baby Gwen's flawless skin. I sat down on the toilet and began to make conversation.

"You want to take a sunbath after a while," I said. "I'm afraid I'll lose my tan."

"Sure," she said. "We can do whatever you want to. Someone called a while ago and asked us to play bridge this afternoon. Do you like to play bridge?"

"I love it," I said. "That's practically all we do in Indiana. We play all the time. My mother plays duplicate. She's got about fifty silver ashtrays she won at tournaments."

"I bet you're really good," she said. She was squirming around while Sirena took her time finishing the other leg.

I lit a cigarette, trying not to look at Baby Gwen's black pubic hair. I had never seen anyone's pubic hair but my own, which was red. It had not occurred to me that there were different colors. "Want a drag?" I asked, handing her the cigarette. She nodded, wiped her hand on her terry-cloth turban, took a long luxurious drag, and French inhaled.

The smoke left her mouth in two little rivers, curled deliciously up over the dark hairs above her lips, and into her nostrils. She held it for a long moment, then exhaled slowly through her lips. The smoke mingled with the sunlight, and the steam coming from the bathwater rose in ragged circles and moved toward the open window.

Baby Gwen rose from the water, her flat body festooned with blossoms of sandalwood soap, and Sirena began to dry her with a towel.

So our life together took shape. In the mornings we sunbathed from 11:00 to 12:00. Thirty minutes on one side and thirty minutes on the other. There were two schools of thought concerning sunbathing. One, that it gave you wrinkles. The other, that it was worth it to look good while you were young.

Baby Gwen and I subscribed to the second theory. Still, we were careful to keep our faces oiled so we wouldn't ruin our complexions. There is no way you could believe how serious we were about such matters. The impenetrable mystery of physical beauty held us like a spell.

In the mornings we spread our blankets in the backyard where a patch of sunlight shone in through the high branches of the elm trees. We covered the blankets with white sheets and set out our supplies, bottles of baby oil, bottles of iodine, alarm clock, eye pads, sunglasses, magazines. We carefully mixed seven drops of iodine with seven ounces of baby oil, shook it for three minutes, then rubbed it on the uncovered parts of each other's bodies. How I loved the feel of Baby Gwen's rib cage under my fingers, the smoothness of her shaved legs. How I dreaded it when her fingers touched the baby fat on my own ribs.

When we were covered with oil we would lie back and

continue our discussion of our romances. I talked of nothing but the ill-fated Bob Aaron, of the songs I would write and dedicate to his memory, of the trip I would take to his deathbed, of the night he drove me home from a football game and let me wear his gloves, of the child I would have by another man and name for him, Robert or Roberta, Bob or Bobbie.

The other thing that fascinated me was the development of my "reputation." I was intensely interested in what people thought of me, in what was being said about me. I set about to develop a reputation in Clarksville as a "madcap," a "wild child," a girl who would do anything. A summer visitor from Washington, D.C., said in my hearing that I reminded him of a young Zelda Fitzgerald and, although I didn't know exactly who Zelda Fitzgerald was, I knew that she had married a writer and drank like a fish and once danced naked in a fountain in Rome. It seemed like a wonderful thing to have said about myself, and I resolved to try to live up to it.

How wonderful it was to be "home," where people knew "who I was," where people thought I was "hilarious" and "crazy" and "just like Leland." I did everything I could think of to feed my new image, becoming very outspoken, saying *damn* and *hell* at every opportunity, wearing dark glasses all the time, even to church. I must have been the first person of normal vision ever to attend the Clarksville Episcopal Church wearing dark glasses.

Baby Gwen's grandmother called every few days to see how we were getting along and once, in a burst of responsibility, came over bringing a dozen pairs of new cotton underpants she had bought for us at the Chinaman's store.

We never could figure out where she got the idea that we were in need of cotton underpants, unless Sirena had mentioned it to her. Perhaps Sirena had tired of hand washing the French lingerie we had taken to wearing every day.

The grandmother had outlived both her daughters and existed in a sort of dreamy half-world with her servants and her religion.

Mostly we kept her satisfied by glowing telephone reports of our popularity and by stopping by occasionally to sit on her porch and have a Coca-Cola.

I fell in love nearly every day with one or the other of the seemingly endless supply of boys who came to call from Drew and Cleveland and Itta Bena and Tutweiler and Rosedale and Leland. Baby Gwen drew boys like honey, and there were always plenty left over to sit around the living room listening to my nonstop conversation.

Boys came by in the evenings, boys called on the telephone, boys invaded our daily bridge games, boys showed up after church, boys took us swimming at the Clarksville Country Club, boys drove us around the cotton fields and down to the river and out to the bootlegger's shack.

The boy I liked best was a good-natured football player named Fielding Reid. Fielding had eyes so blue and hair so blonde and shoulders so wide and teased me so unmercifully about my accent that I completely forgot he was the steady boyfriend of Clarice Fitzhugh, who was off on a trip to Mexico with her family. Fielding had taken to hanging around Baby Gwen and me while he waited for Clarice's return.

He loved to kibitz on our bridge games, eating all the mints and pecans from the little dishes and leaning over my shoulder cheering me on. In the afternoons we played endless polite bridge games, so different from the bitter hard-fought bridge I had played in the forgotten state of Indiana.

Although I was an erratic and unpredictable bidder, I was a sought-after partner for I held good cards and nearly always won.

There was a girl from Drew named Sarah who came over several afternoons a week to play with us. She was Fielding's cousin and she had a wooden arm painted the color of her skin. It was not a particularly well made arm, and the paint was peeling in several places on the hand. She was pleasant enough looking otherwise and had nice clothes with loose sleeves that hid the place where the false arm joined the real one.

I made a great show of being nice to Sarah, lighting her cigarettes, asking her opinion about things, letting her be my bridge partner. She was delighted with the attention I gave her and was always telling someone how "wonderful" I was and how much it meant to her to have me in Clarksville.

The wrist and fingers of Sarah's false arm were hinged and she could move the joints with her good hand and lock them in place. She was in the habit of holding the wooden arm in front of her when she was seated at the bridge table. Then she would place her bridge hand in the wooden fingers and play out of it with her good hand.

Of course, anyone sitting on either side of her could see her cards by the slightest movement of their eyes. It took a lot of pressure off me when she was my partner.

Fielding thought I was "wonderful" too. He went around saying I was his "partner" and took me into his confidence, even telling me his fears that the absent Clarice Fitzhugh was being unfaithful to him in Mexico. That she might be "using" him.

Don't worry, I assured him. Clarice was a great girl. She wouldn't use anyone. He must trust her and not listen to idle gossip. Everything would be fine when she got home, and so forth. Part of my new reputation was that "LeLe never says a bad word about anyone," "LeLe always looks on the bright side," "everyone feels like they've known LeLe all their lives," "you can tell LeLe *anything.*"

I was beginning to believe my own publicity, that I was someone very special, that there might be some special destiny in store for me.

Several times that summer I was filled with an elation so powerful and overwhelming that it felt as though my body were leaving the earth. This always happened at night, when I was alone in the yard, caught in the shadow of the Nandina bushes which covered the side of the house like bright dark clouds. I remember standing in the starlight filled with some inexpressible joy. It would become very intense, like music. I was terribly excited by these feelings and could not bring myself to speak of them, even to Baby Gwen.

Often that summer I was given to seizures of abrupt excitement while I was dressing. I would catch a glimpse of myself in a mirror and burst into laughter, or, deciding for a moment that I was pretty, begin to tremble and jump up and go dancing around the room.

I had a recurrent dream that summer. I dreamed that I was walking through our old house in Indiana and I would notice that the dining room opened up into rooms and rooms I had not known existed, strange and oddly shaped rooms full of heavy furniture, expensive dusty dressers with drawers full of treasures, old gowns and sweaters and capes, jewels and letters and old documents, wills and deeds and diaries. These rooms opened onto patios and sun porches and solariums, and I saw that we were wealthy people. I wanted to run back and find my parents and tell them what I had found, but my curiosity drove me forward. I had to keep opening doors until I knew the extent of our riches, so I kept on moving through the strange rooms until I woke.

One morning Fielding came by unexpectedly and asked me to go with him to see about some repairs for his car. We left it with a mechanic at the filling station and walked to the Mayflower Café, a place on the square where farmers and merchants gathered in the mornings for coffee and gossip. I had never been alone in a restaurant with a boy, and I was excited and began talking very fast to cover my excitement. I ordered doughnuts and began turning my turquoise ring around on my finger so the waitress would think it was a wedding band.

"I've been wanting to talk to you alone," Fielding said.

"Sure," I said, choking on a powdered doughnut. It was all too wonderful, sitting in a booth so early in the morning with a really good-looking boy.

"LeLe," he said, smiling at me and reaching across the table to hold my hand. There was his garnet class ring, blazing at me from the tabletop. At any moment it might be mine. I could scarcely breathe. "LeLe," he repeated, "I don't want you to get me wrong when I say this. I don't want to hurt your feelings or anything, but, well, I really want to tell you something." He squeezed my hand tighter. "LeLe, you would be a really beautiful girl if you lost ten pounds, do you know that? Because you have a beautiful face. I'm only saying this because we've gotten to be such good friends and I thought I ought..."

I was stunned. But I recovered. "I'm not really this fat," I said. "At home I'm a cheerleader and I'm on the swimming team and I'm very thin. But last year the boy I love got cancer and I've been having a lot of trouble with my thyroid since then. The doctors think there may be something wrong with my thyroid or my metabolism. I may have to have an operation pretty soon."

"Oh, LeLe," he said. "I didn't know it was anything like that. I thought maybe you ate too much or something." He reached out and took my other hand. I was still holding part of a doughnut.

"Don't worry about it, Fielding. How could you know. You didn't hurt my feelings. Besides, I don't mind. The operation may not be so bad. It isn't like having polio or something they can't fix. At least I have something they can fix."

"Oh, LeLe."

"Don't worry about it. And don't tell anyone about it, even Baby Gwen. I don't want people feeling sorry for me. So it's a secret."

"Don't worry, LeLe. I'll never tell anyone. Are you sure it'll be all right? About the operation I mean?"

"Oh, sure. I might not even have to have it. My thyroid might get better all by itself."

After that Fielding and I were closer than ever. I began to halfway believe the part about the thyroid trouble. My mother was always talking about her thyroid and taking some sort of little white pill for it.

Late one afternoon Baby Gwen and I were sitting on the porch swing talking to Fielding. It was one of those days in August when you can smell autumn in the air, a feeling of change coming over the world. I had won at bridge that afternoon. I had made seven hearts doubled and redoubled with Fielding looking over my shoulder, and I was filled with a sense of power.

"Let's all go swimming tomorrow," I said. "They'll be closing the pool soon and I need to practice my strokes."

"Let's go to the lake," Fielding said. "I haven't made my summer swim across the lake. I was waiting for Russell to get home, but I don't guess he'll be back in time so I might as well go on and swim it myself."

"I'll swim it with you," I heard myself saying. "I'm a Junior Red Cross Lifesaver. I can swim forever."

"You couldn't swim this," he said. "It's five miles."

"I can swim a lot further than that," I said. "I practically taught swimming at camp. I never got tired."

"What about your . . . you know . . . your condition?"

"That's all right," I said. "Exercise is good for me. I'm supposed to go swimming all I can. The doctors said it was the best thing I could do."

Baby Gwen looked puzzled. "You can't swim all the way across the lake without a boat," she said. "Girls don't ever swim across the lake."

"I can swim it," I said, "I've been further than that at camp lots of times. What time you want to go, Fielding?"

By the time he came to pick us up the next morning I had calmed Baby Gwen down and convinced her there was nothing to worry about. I really was a good swimmer. Swimming was of no importance to me one way or the other. What mattered to me was that a boy of my own choosing, a first-rate boy, was coming to take me somewhere. Not coming for Baby Gwen and taking me along to be nice, but *coming for me.*

I had been awake since dawn deciding what to wear. I finally settled on my old green Jantzen and a white blouse from Big Gwen's wardrobe. The blouse had little shoulder pads and big chunky buttons and fell across my shoulders and arms in soft pleats. I wasn't worried at all about swimming the lake. The only thing that worried me was whether the blouse was long enough to cover my stomach.

Baby Gwen went with us. As soon as we left the shore she was supposed to drive around to the other side and watch for us. All the way out to the lake she sat beside me looking worried.

"You ought to have a boat going along beside you," she said.

"We don't need a boat," I said. "I'm a Junior Red Cross Lifesaver. I can swim all day if I want."

"It's O.K.," Fielding said. "Russell and I do it every summer."

By the time we got to the lake I felt like I could swim the Atlantic Ocean. The sun was brilliant on the blue water, and as soon as Fielding stopped the car I jumped out and ran down to the shore and looked out across the water to the pine trees on the far shore. It didn't look so far away, only very blue and deep and mysterious. I took off my blouse and shoes and waded out into the water. How clean it felt, how cool. I put my face down and touched my cheek to the water. I felt the water across my legs and stomach. My body felt wonderful and light in the water. I rose up on my toes and my legs felt strong and tall. I pulled in my stomach until my ribs stuck out. I was beautiful. I was perfect. I began to throw handfuls of water up into the air. The water caught in the sunlight and fell back all around me. I threw more into the air and it fell all around me, falling in pieces of steel and glass and diamonds, diamonds falling all around me. I called out, "Come on, Fielding. Either we're swimming across this lake or we aren't."

"Wait," he called back. "Wait up." Then he was beside me in the water and I felt his hands around my waist and the pressure of his knee against my thigh. "Let's go then," he said in a low sweet voice. "Let's do this together."

Then we began to swim out, headed for the stand of pine and oak and cypress on the far shore.

The time passed as if in a dream. My arms moved easily, taking turns pulling the soft yielding water alongside my body. I was counting out the strokes, one, two, three, four, five, six, seven, eight, one, two, three, four, five, six, seven, eight . . . over and over in the good old-fashioned Australian crawl. Every now and then Fielding would touch my arm and we would roll over on our backs and rest for a few minutes, checking our position. Then we would swim for a while on our sides, resting. There were long banks of clouds on the horizon and far overhead a great hawk circling like a black planet. Everytime I looked up he was there.

We swam for what seemed to be a long, long time, but whenever I looked ahead the trees on the shore never seemed to come any closer.

"Are you sure we're going in a straight line," I said, when we turned over to rest for a moment.

"I think so," Fielding said. "The current might be pulling us a little to the left. There's nothing we can do about it now anyway."

"Why," I said. "Why can't we do anything about it?"

"Well, we can't go back," he said. "We're past the point of no return."

The point of no return I said to myself. Maybe we would die out here and they would change the name of the lake in honor of us. Lake LeLe, Lake Leland Louise Arnold, Lover's Lake. "Don't worry about it then," I said. "Just keep on swimming."

Perhaps an hour went by, perhaps two. The sun was hot on the water, and every now and then a breeze blew up. Once a barge carrying logs to the sawmill passed us without noticing us. We treaded water while it passed and then rocked in the wake for several minutes. They had passed us as though we didn't exist. After the barge went by we began to swim with more determination. I was beginning to feel cold, but it didn't seem to really matter. Nothing mattered but this boy and the sun and the clouds and the great hawk circling and the water touching me everywhere. I put down my head and began to count with renewed vigor, one, two, three, four, five, six, seven, eight, one, two, three, four, . . .

"LeLe," Fielding called out. "LeLe, put your feet down. Put your feet down, LeLe." I looked up and he was standing a few feet away holding his hands up in the air. I let my feet drop and my toes touched the cool flat sand. We were on the sandbar. Then we were laughing and hugging and holding on to each other and moving toward the shore where Baby Gwen stood calling and calling to us. It was wonderful, wonderful, wonderful, wonderful. I was wonderful. I was dazzling. I was LeLe Arnold, the wildest girl in the Mississippi Delta, the girl who swam Lake Jefferson without a boat or a life vest. I was LeLe, the girl who would do anything.

All the way home in the car Fielding kept his arm around me while he drove and Baby Gwen fed me little pieces of the picnic lunch and I was happier than I had ever been in my life and I might have stayed that way forever but when we got home there was a message saying that my parents were on their way to Clarksville to take me home.

My parents. I had forgotten they existed. My father had gotten lonely and driven to New Orleans and talked my mother into coming home.

Later that afternoon they arrived. It seemed strange to see our Buick pulling up in Baby Gwen's driveway. My father got out looking very young and my mother was holding on to his arm. She looked like a stranger, thin and beautiful in a black cotton peasant dress with rows of colored rickrack around the hem and sleeves. Her hair was cut short and curled around her face in ringlets. I was almost afraid to touch her. Then she ran from my father's side and grabbed me in her arms and whirled me around and around and I smelled the delicate perfume on her skin and it made me feel like crying.

When she put me down I turned to my father. "I'm not going home," I said, putting my hands on my hips.

"Oh, yes you are," he said, so I went upstairs and began to pack my clothes.

Baby Gwen followed me up the stairs. "You can have the kimono," she said. "I want you to have it." She folded it carefully and packed it with tissue paper in a box from Nell's and Blum's and put it beside my suitcase.

"Come sit by me, Baby Gwen, and tell me the news," my mother said, and Baby Gwen went over and sat by her on the chaise. My mother put her arms around her and began to talk in a bright voice inviting her to spend Christmas with us in Indiana.

"It will snow for sure," my mother said. "And LeLe can show you the snow."

We left Clarksville early the next morning. Baby Gwen stood in the doorway waving good-bye. She was wearing a pink satin robe stained in places from where she had sweated in it during the hot nights of July, and her little nipples stuck out beneath the soft material.

I kept hoping maybe Fielding had gotten up early to come and tell me goodbye, but he didn't make it.

"I'll fix those hems when she comes to visit," my mother said, "and do something about that perfume."

I was too tired to argue. All the way to Indiana I slumped in the back seat eating potato chips and sneaking smokes in filling-station restrooms when we stopped for gas.

Then it was another morning and I woke up in my old room and put on my shorts and rode my bicycle over to Cynthia Carver's house. She was in the basement doing her

Saturday morning ironing. Cynthia hated to iron. How many mornings had I sat on those basement steps watching the forlorn look on her face while she finished her seven blouses.

"So I might as well be dead," I said, taking a bite of a cookie. "So, anyway, I wish I was dead," I repeated, as Cynthia hung a blouse on a hanger and started on a dirndl skirt. "Here I am, practically engaged to this rich plantation owner's son... Fielding. Fielding Reid, LeLe Reid... so, anyway, my mother and father come and drag me home practically the same day we fell in love. I don't know how they got wind of it unless that damn Sirena called and told them. She was always watching everything I did. Anyway, they drag me home and I bet they won't even let him write to me."

"What's that perfume?" Cynthia said, lifting her eyes from the waistband of the skirt.

"That's my signature," I said. "That's what I wear now. Tigress in the winter and Aprodisia in the summer. That's what this writer's wife always wore. She got pneumonia or something from swimming in the winter and died when she was real young. Everyone in Clarksville thinks I'm just like her. She was from Mississippi or something. I think she's sort of my father's cousin."

Cynthia pulled the dirndl off the ironing board and began on a pair of pedal pushers. I leaned back on the stairs, watching the steam from the pedal pushers light up the space over Cynthia Carver's disgruntled Yankee head. I was dreaming of the lake, trying to remember how the water turned into diamonds in my hands.

Summer, an Elegy

His name was Shelby after the town where his mother was born, and he was eight years old and all that summer he had to wear a little black sling around the index finger of his right hand. He had to wear the sling because his great-granddaddy had been a famous portrait painter and had paintings hanging in the White House.

Shelby was so high-strung his mother was certain he was destined to be an artist like his famous ancestor. So, when he broke his finger and it grew back crooked, of couse they took him to a specialist. They weren't taking any chances on a deformity standing in his way.

All summer long he was supposed to wear the sling to limber up the finger, and in the fall the doctor was going to operate and straighten it. While he waited for his operation Shelby was brought to Bear Garden Plantation to spend the summer with his grandmother, and as soon as he got up every morning he rode over to Esperanza to look for Matille.

He would come riding up in the yard and tie his saddle pony to the fence and start talking before he even got on the porch. He was a beautiful boy, five months younger than Matille, and he was the biggest liar she had ever met in her life.

Matille was the only child in a house full of widows. She was glad of this noisy companion fate had delivered to Issaquena County right in the middle of a World War.

Shelby would wait for her while she ate breakfast, helping himself to pinch-cake, or toast, or cold cornbread, or muffins, walking around the kitchen touching everything and talking a mile a minute to anyone who would listen, talking and eating at the same time.

"My daddy's a personal friend of General MacArthur's," he would be saying. "They were buddies at Auburn. General MacArthur wants him to come work in Washington, but he can't go because what he does is too important." Shelby was standing in the pantry door making a pyramid out of the Campbell Soup cans. "Every time my daddy talks about going to Washington my momma starts crying her head off and goes to bed with a headache." He topped off the pyramid with a can of tomato paste and returned to the present. "I don't know how anyone can sleep this late," he said, "I'm the first one up at Bear Garden every single morning."

Matille would eat breakfast as fast as she could and they would start out for the bayou that ran in front of the house at the end of a wide lawn.

"Did I tell you I'm engaged to be married," Shelby would begin, sitting next to Matille in the swing that went out over the water, pumping as hard as he could with his thin legs, staring off into the sky.

"Her daddy's a colonel in the air corps. They're real rich." A dark, secret look crossed his face. "I already gave her a diamond ring. That's why I've got to find the pearl. So I can get enough money to get married. But don't tell anyone because my momma and daddy don't know about it yet."

"There aren't any pearls in mussels," Matille said. "Guy said so. He said we were wasting our time chopping open all those mussels."

"They do too have pearls," Shelby said coldly. "Better ones than oysters. My father told me all about it. Everyone in New Orleans knows about it."

"Well," Matille said, "I'm not looking for any pearls today. I'm going to the store and play the slot machine."

"You haven't got any nickels."

"I can get one. Guy'll give me one." Guy was Matille's uncle. He was 4-F. He had lost an eye in a crop-dusting accident and was having to miss the whole war because of it. He couldn't get into the army, navy, marines, or air corps. Even the coast guard had turned him down. He tried to keep up a cheerful face, running around Esperanza doing the work of three men, being extra nice to everyone, even the German war prisoners who were brought over from the Greenville Air Force Base to work in the fields.

He was always good for a nickel, sometimes two or three if Matille waited until after he had his evening toddies.

"If you help me with the mussels I'll give you two nickels," Shelby said.

"Let me see," Matille said, dragging her feet to slow the swing. It was nice in the swing with the sun beating down on the water below and the pecan trees casting a cool shade.

Shelby pulled a handkerchief from his pocket and untied a corner. Sure enough, there they were, three nickels and a quarter and a dime. Shelby always had money. He was the richest boy Matille had even known. She stared down at the nickels, imagining the cold thrill of the slot machine handle throbbing beneath her touch.

"How long?" she said.

"Until I have to go home," Shelby said.

"All right," Matille said. "Let's get started."

They went out to the shed and found two rakes and a small hoe and picked their way through the weeds to the bayou bank. The mud along the bank was black and hard-packed and broken all along the waterline by thick tree roots, cypress and willow and catalpa and water oak. They walked past the cleared-off place with its pier and rope swings and on down to where the banks of mussels began.

The mussels lay in the shallow water as far as the rake could reach, an endless supply, as plentiful as oak leaves, as plentiful as the fireflies that covered the lawn at evening, as plentiful as the minnows casting their tiny shadows all along the water's edge, or the gnats that buzzed around Matille's face as she worked, raking and digging and chopping, earning her nickels.

She would throw the rake down into the water and pull it back full of the dark-shelled, inedible, mud-covered creatures. Moments later, reaching into the same place, dozens more would have appeared to take their place.

They would rake in a pile of mussels, then set to work breaking them open with the hoe and screwdriver. When they had opened twenty or thirty, they would sit on the bank searching the soft flesh for the pearl. Behind them and all around them were piles of rotting shells left behind in the past weeks.

"I had my fortune told by a voodoo queen last Mardi

Gras," Shelby said. "Did I ever tell you about that? She gave me a charm made out of a dead baby's bone. You want to see it?"

"I been to Ditty's house and had my fortune told," Matille said. "Ditty's real old. She's the oldest person in Issaquena County. She's older than Nannie-Mother. She's probably the oldest person in the whole state of Mississippi." Matille picked up a mussel and examined it, running her finger inside, then tossed it into the water. Where it landed a dragonfly hovered for a moment, then rose in the humid air, its electric-blue tail flashing.

"You want to see the charm or not?" Shelby said, pulling it out of his pocket.

"Sure," she said. "Give it here."

He opened his hand and held it out to her. It looked like the wishbone from a tiny chicken. "It's voodoo," Shelby said. He held it up in the air, turning it to catch the sunlight. "You can touch it but you can't hold it. No one can hold it but the master of it. Here, go on and touch it if you want to."

Matille reached out and stroked the little bone. "What's it good for?" she asked.

"To make whatever you want to happen. It's white magic. Momma Ulaline is real famous. She's got a place on Royal Street right next to an antique store. My Aunt Katherine took me there when she was baby-sitting me last Mardi Gras."

Matille touched it again. She gave a little shudder.

"Well, let's get back to work," Shelby said, putting the charm into his pocket, wiping his hands on his playsuit. His little black sling was covered with mud. "I think we're getting someplace today. I think we're getting warm."

They went back to work. Shelby was quiet, dreaming of treasure, of the pearl that lay in wait for him, of riches beyond his wildest dreams, of mansions and fine automobiles and chauffeurs and butlers and maids and money, stacks and stacks of crisp five-dollar bills and ten-dollar bills and twenty-dollar bills. Somewhere in Steele's Bayou the pearl waited. It loomed in his dreams. It lay in wait for him beneath the roots of a cypress or water oak or willow.

Every morning when he woke he could see it, all morning as he dug and raked and chopped and Matille complained and the hot sun beat down on the sweating mud and the stagnant pools of minnows and the fast-moving, evil-looking gars swimming by like gunboats, all day the pearl shone in his mind, smooth and mysterious, cold to the touch.

They worked in silence for awhile, moving downstream until they were almost to the bridge.

"Looks like we could get something for all these shells," Matille said, examining the inside of one. It was all swirls of pink and white, like polished marble. "Looks like they ought to be worth something!"

"We could make dog food out of the insides," Shelby said. "Mr. Green Bagett had a dog that ate mussels. My grandmother told me all about it. He would carry them up to the road in his mouth and when the sun made them open he would suck out the insides." Shelby leaned on his hoe, making a loud sucking noise. "He was a dog named Harry after Mr. Bagett's dentist and he would eat mussels all day long if nobody stopped him."

"Why don't we carry these mussels up to the road and let the sun open them?" Matille said.

"Because it takes too long that way," Shelby said. "This is quicker."

"We could make ashtrays out of the shells," Matille said.

"Yeah," Shelby said. "We could sell them in New Orleans. You can sell anything in the French Quarter."

"We could paint them and decorate them with flowers," Matille said, falling into a dream of her own, picturing herself wearing a long flowered dress, pushing a cart through the crowded streets of a city, selling ashtrays to satisfied customers.

Now they were almost underneath the bridge. Here the trees were thicker and festooned with vines that dropped into the water like swings. It was darker here, and secret.

The bridge was a fine one for such a small bayou. It was a drawbridge with high steel girders that gleamed like silver in the flat Delta countryside. The bridge had been built to connect the two parts of the county, and anyone going from Grace to Baleshed or Esperanza or Panther Brake or Greenfields had to pass that way. Some mornings as many as seven cars and trucks passed over it. All day small black children played on the bridge and fished from it and leaned over its railings looking down into the brown water, chunking rocks at the mud turtles or trying to hit the mean-looking gars and catfish that swam by in twos or threes with their teeth showing.

This morning there were half a dozen little black boys on the bridge and one little black girl wearing a clean apron. Her hair was in neat cornrows with yellow yarn plaited into the braids. Her head looked like the wing of a butterfly, all yellow and black and brown and round as it could be.

"What y'all doing?" the girl called down when they got close enough to hear. "What y'all doing to them mussels?"

"We're doing an experiment," Shelby called back.

"Let's get Teentsy and Kale to help us," Matille said. "Hey, Teentsy," she called out, but Shelby grabbed her arm.

"Don't get them down here," he said. "I don't want everyone in the Delta in on this."

"They all know about it anyway," Matille said. "Guy told Granddaddy everyone at the store was laughing about us the other day. He said Baby Doll was busting a gut laughing at us for chopping all these mussels."

"I don't care," Shelby said, putting his hands on his hips, looking out across the water with the grim resignation of the born artist. "They don't know what we're doing it for."

"Well, I'm about worn out," Matille said. "Let's go up to the store and get Mavis to give us a drink."

"Let's open a few more first. Then we'll get a drink and go over to the other side. I think it's better over there anyway. There's sand over there. You got to have sand to make pearls."

"We can't go over there," Matille said. "That's not our property. That's Mr. Donleavy's place."

"He don't care if we dig some mussels on his bayou bank, does he?"

"I don't know. We got to ask him first. He's got a real bad temper."

"Let's try under this tree," Shelby said. "This looks like a good place. There's sand in this mud." He was bending down, trying the mud between his fingers, rubbing it back and forth to test the consistency. "Yeah, let's try here. This feels good."

"What y'all tearing up all those mussels for," Kale called down from his perch on the bridge. "They ain't good for nothing. You can't even use them for bait."

"We're gonna make ashtrays out of them," Shelby said. "We're starting us an ashtray factory."

"Where about?" Kale said, getting interested, looking like he would come down and take a look for himself.

"Next to the store," Shelby said. "We're gonna decorate them and sell them in New Orleans. Rich folks will pay a lot for real mussel ashtrays."

"That ought to hold them for a while," he said to Matille. "Let them talk about that at the store. Come on, let's open a few more. Then we'll get us a drink."

"All right," Matille said. "Let's try under this tree." She waded out into the water until it was up to her ankles, feeling the cold mud ooze up between her toes. She reached out with the rake. It caught, and she began pulling it up the shore, backing as she pulled, tearing the bark off the edges of the tree roots. The rake caught in the roots, and she reached down to free it.

"Matille!" Shelby yelled. "Matille! Look out!" She heard his voice and saw the snake at the same moment, saw the snake and Shelby lifting the hoe and her hand outlined against the water, frozen and dappled with sunlight and the snake struggling to free itself and the hoe falling toward her hand, and she dropped the rake and turned and was running up the bank, stumbling and running, with Shelby yelling his head off behind her, and Teentsy and Kale and the other children rose up from the bridge like a flock of little blackbirds and came running down the hill to see what the excitement was.

"I got him," Shelby yelled. "I cut him in two. I cut him in two with the hoe. I got him."

Matille sank down on the edge of the road and put her head on her knees.

"She's fainting," Kale called out, running up to her. "Matille's fainting."

"No, she ain't," Teentsy said. "She's all right." Teentsy sat down by Matille and put a hand on her arm, patting her.

"It was a moccasin," Shelby yelled. "He was big around as

my arm. After I killed him the top half was still alive. He struck at me four times. I don't know if I'm bit or not."

"Where's he gone to now?" Kale said.

"I don't know," Shelby said, pulling off his shirt. "Come look and see if he bit me." The children gathered around searching Shelby's skin for bite marks. His little chest was heaving with excitement and his face was shining. With his shirt off he looked about as big around as a blue jay. His little black sling was flopping around his wrist and his rib cage rose and fell beneath the straps of his seersucker playsuit.

"Here's one!" Teentsy screamed, touching a spot on Shelby's back, but it turned out to be an old mosquito bite.

"Lay down on the ground," Kale yelled, "where we can look at you better."

"Where do you *think* he bit you?" Teentsy said.

But Shelby was too excited to lay down on the ground. All he wanted to do was jump up and down and tell his story over and over.

Then the grown people heard the commotion and came out from the store. Mavis Findley and Mr. Beaumont and Baby Doll and R. C. and Overflow came hurrying down the road and grabbed hold of Shelby so they could see where the snake bit him.

"Didn't nothing bite him, Mr. Mavis," Kale said. "He kilt it. He kilt it with the hoe."

"He almost chopped my hand off," Matille said, but no one was listening.

Then Mavis and Baby Doll and Overflow escorted Matille and Shelby back to the big house with the black children skipping along beside and in front of them like a disorderly marching band.

By the time the procession reached the house the porch was full of ladies. Matille's mother and grandmother and great-grandmother and several widowed aunts had materialized from their rooms and were standing in a circle. From a distance they looked like a great flowering shrub. The screen door was open and a wasp buzzed around their heads threatening to be caught in their hairnets.

The ladies all began talking at once, their voices rising

161

above and riding over and falling into each other in a long chorus of mothering.

"Thank goodness you're all in one piece," Miss Babbie said, swooping up Matille and enfolding her in a cool fragrance of dotted Swiss and soft yielding bosom and the smell of sandalwood and the smell of coffee and the smell of powder.

Miss Nannie-Mother, who was ninety-six, kissed her on the forehead and called her Eloise, after a long-dead cousin. Miss Nannie-Mother had lived so long and grown so wise that everyone in the world had started to look alike to her.

The rest of the ladies swirled around Shelby. Matille struggled from her grandmother's embrace and watched disgustedly from the door frame as Shelby told his story for the tenth time.

"I didn't care what happened to me," Shelby was saying. "No rattlesnake was biting a lady while I was in the neighborhood. After I chopped it in two the mouth part came at me like a chicken with its head cut off."

"He almost chopped my hand off," Matille said again, but the only ones listening to her were Teentsy and Kale, who stood by the steps picking petals off Miss Teddy's prize pansies and covering their mouths with their hands when they giggled to show what nice manners they had.

"This is what comes of letting children run loose like wild Indians," Miss Teddy was saying, brandishing a bottle of Windsor nail polish.

"Whatever will Rhoda Hotchkiss think when she hears of this?" Miss Grace said.

"She'll be terrified," Miss Babbie answered. "Then go straight to her knees and thank the Lord for the narrow escape."

"I knew something was going to happen," Miss Hannie Clay said, her hands full of rickrack for the smock she was making for her daughter in Shreveport. "I knew something was coming. It was too quiet around here all morning if you ask my opinion."

Matille leaned into the door frame with her hands on her hips watching her chances of ever going near the bayou again as long as she lived growing slimmer and slimmer.

Sure enough, when Matille's grandfather came in from the fields for the noon meal he made his pronouncement before he even washed his hands or hung up his hat.

"Well, then," he said, looking down from his six feet four inches and furrowing his brow. "I want everyone in this house to stay away from the bayou until I can spare some men to clear the brush. Shelby, I'm counting on you to keep Matille away from there, you hear me?"

"Yes sir," Shelby said. He stood up very straight, stuck out his hand, and shook on it.

Now he's done it Matille thought. Now nothing will be the same.

Now the summer wore on into August, and Shelby and Matille made a laboratory in an old chicken house and collected a lot of butterflies and chloroformed them with fingernail polish remover, and they taught a fox terrier puppy how to dance on his hind legs, and spent some time spying on the German prisoners, and read all the old love letters in the trunks under the house, but it was not the same. Somehow the heart had gone out of the summer.

Then one morning the grown people decided it was time for typhoid shots, and no matter how Matille cried and beat her head against the floor she was bathed and dressed and sent off in the back seat of Miss Rhoda's Buick to Doctor Findley's little brick office overlooking Lake Washington.

As a reward Matille was to be allowed to stay over at Bear Garden until the pain and fever subsided.

In those days vaccinations were much stronger than they are now and well-cared-for children were kept in bed for twenty-four hours nursing their sore arms, taking aspirin dissolved in sugar water, and being treated as though they were victims of the disease itself.

Miss Rhoda made up the twin beds in Shelby's mother's old room, made them up with her finest Belgian linens and decorated the headboards with Hero medals cut from cardboard and hand painted with watercolors.

The bedroom was painted ivory and the chairs were covered with blue and white chintz imported from Paris. It was the finest room Matille had ever slept in. She snuggled down in the pillows admiring the tall bookcases filled with old dolls and momentos of Carrie Hotchkiss's brilliant career as a Rolling Fork cheerleader.

Miss Rhoda bathed their faces with lemon water, drew the Austrian blinds, and went off for her nap.

"Does yours hurt yet?" Shelby asked, rubbing his shot as hard as he could to get the pain going. "Mine's killing me already."

"It hurts some," Matille said, touching the swollen area. "Not too much." She was looking at Shelby's legs, remembering something that had happened a long time ago, something hot and exciting, something that felt like fever, and like fever, made everything seem present, always present, so that she could not remember where or how it had happened or how long a time had passed since she had forgotten it.

"Just wait till tonight," Shelby rattled on. "You'll think your arm's fixing to fall off. I almost died from mine last year. One year a boy in New Orleans did die. They cut off his arm and did everything they could to save him but he died anyway. Think about that, being in a grave with only one arm." Shelby was talking faster than ever, to hide his embarrassment at the way Matille was looking at him.

"I can't stand to think about being buried, can you?" he continued, "all shut up in the ground with the worms eating you. I'm getting buried in a mausoleum if I die. They're these little houses up off the ground made out of concrete. Everyone in New Orleans that can afford it gets buried in mausoleums. That's one good thing about living there."

"You want to get in bed with me?" Matille said, surprised at the sound of her own voice, clear and orderly in the still room.

"Sure," Shelby said, "if you're scared. It scares me to death to think about being buried and stuff like that. Are you scared?"

"I don't know," Matille said. "I just feel funny. I feel like doing something bad."

"Well, scoot over then," Shelby said, crawling in beside her.

"You're burning up," she said, putting a hand on his forehead to see if he had a fever. Then she put her hand on his chest as if to feel his heartbeat, and then, as if she had been doing it every day of her life, she reached down inside his pajamas for the strange hard secret of boys.

"I want to see it, Shelby," she said, and he lay back with

his hands stiff by his sides while she touched and looked to her heart's content.

"Now you do it to me," she said, and she guided his fingers up and down, up and down the thick wet opening between her legs.

The afternoon went on for a long time, and the small bed was surrounded by yellow light and the room filled with the smell of mussels.

Long afterward, as she lay in a cool bed in Acapulco, waiting for her third husband to claim her as his bride, Matille would remember that light and how, later that afternoon, the wind picked up and could be heard for miles away, moving toward Issaquena County with its lines of distant thunder, and how the cottonwood leaves outside the window had beat upon the house all night with their exotic crackling.

"You better not tell anyone about this ever, Shelby," Matille said, when she woke in the morning. "You can't tell anyone about it, not even in New Orleans."

"The moon's still up," Shelby said, as if he hadn't heard her. "I can see it out the window."

"How can the moon be up," Matille said. "It's daylight."

"It stays up when it wants to," Shelby said. "Haven't you ever seen that before."

That was the beginning. They cleared out an old playhouse that had belonged to Matille's mother and made a bed from an old cot mattress.

It was Matille who made up the game now. She would lie down on the mattress with her hand on her head pretending to have a sick headache.

"Come sit by me, Honey," she would say. "Pour me a glass of sherry and come lie down till I feel better."

"God can see in this playhouse," Shelby said, pulling his hand away.

"No, he can't, Shelby," Matille said, sitting up and looking him hard in the eye. "God can't see through tin. This is a tin roof and God can't see through it."

"He can see everywhere," Shelby said. "Father Godchaux said so."

"Well, he can't see through tin," Matille said. "He can't be

165

everywhere at once. He's got enough to do helping out the Allies without watching little boys and girls every minute of the night and day." Matille was unbuttoning Shelby's playsuit. "Doesn't that feel good, Shelby," she said. "Doesn't that make it feel better."

"God can see everywhere," Shelby insisted. "He can see every single thing in the whole world."

"I don't care," Matille said. "I don't like God anyway. If God's so good why did he let Uncle Robert die. And why did he make alligators and snakes and send my daddy off to fight the Japs. If God's so good why'd he let the Jews kill his own little boy."

"You better not talk like that," Shelby said, buttoning his suit back together. "And we better get back before Baby Doll comes looking for us again."

"Just a little bit more," Matille said. "Just till we get to the part where the baby comes out."

August went by as if it had only lasted a moment. Then one afternoon Miss Rhoda drove Shelby over in the Buick to say good-bye. He was wearing long pants and had a clean sling on the finger and he had brought Matille the voodoo bone wrapped in tissue paper to keep for him.

"You might need this," he said, holding it out to her. He looked very grown-up standing by the stairs in his city clothes, and Matille thought that maybe she would marry Shelby when she grew up and be a fine married lady in New Orleans.

Then it was September and the cotton went to the gin and Matille was in the third grade and rode to school on the bus.

One afternoon she was standing by the driver while the bus clattered across the bridge and came to a halt by the store. It was a cool day. A breeze was blowing from the northeast and the cypress trees were turning a dusty red and the wild persimmons and muscadines were making.

Matille felt the trouble before she even got off the bus. The trouble reached out and touched her before she even saw the ladies standing on the porch in their dark dresses. It fell across her shoulders like a cloak. It was as if she had

touched a strand of a web and felt the whole thing tremble and knew herself to be caught forever in its trembling.

They found out, she thought. Shelby told them. Now
they'll kill me. Now they'll beat me like they did Guy.

She looked down the gravel road to the house, down the
long line of pecan and elm trees and knew that she should
turn and go back the other way, should run from this trouble,
but something made her keep on moving toward the house.
I'll say he lied, she thought. I'll say I didn't do it. I'll say he
made it up. Everyone knows what a liar Shelby is.

Then her mother and grandmother and Miss Babbie came
down off the porch and took her into the parlor and sat beside
her on the sofa. And Miss Hannie and Miss Nell Grace and
Overflow and Baby Doll stood around her in a circle and told
her the terrible news.

"Shelby is dead, Matille," her grandmother said, and the
words slid over her like water falling on stones.

Shelby had gone to the hospital to have his finger fixed and
he had lain down on the table and put the gas mask over his
face and the man who ran the machine made a mistake and
Shelby had gone to sleep and nothing could wake him up,
not all the screams or shots or slaps in the face or prayers or
remorse in the world could wake him. And that was the
Lord's will, blessed be the name of the Lord, Amen.

Later the ladies went into the kitchen to make a cold
supper for anyone who felt like eating and Matille walked
down to the bayou and stood for a long time staring down into
the water, feeling strangely elated, as though this were some
wonderful joke Shelby had dreamed up.

She stared down into the tree roots, deep down into the
muddy water, down to the place where Shelby's pearl
waited, grew and moved inside the soft watery flesh of its
mother, luminous and perfect and alive, as cold as the moon
in the winter sky.

$\mathcal{V}$OICES OF THE $\mathcal{S}$OUTH

Hamilton Basso
  *The View from Pompey's
    Head*
Richard Bausch
  Real Presence
  Take Me Back
Robert Bausch
  On the Way Home
Doris Betts
  *The Astronomer and
    Other Stories*
  *The Gentle Insurrection
    and Other Stories*
Sheila Bosworth
  Almost Innocent
  Slow Poison
David Bottoms
  Easter Weekend
Erskine Caldwell
  Poor Fool
Fred Chappell
  Dagon
  The Gaudy Place
  The Inkling
  It Is Time, Lord
Kelly Cherry
  Augusta Played
Vicki Covington
  Bird of Paradise
Elizabeth Cox
  *The Ragged Way People
    Fall Out of Love*
R. H. W. Dillard
  The Book of Changes
Ellen Douglas
  A Family's Affairs
  A Lifetime Burning
  The Rock Cried Out
  Where the Dreams Cross
Percival Everett
  Cutting Lisa
  Suder
Peter Feibleman
  *The Daughters of
    Necessity*
  A Place Without Twilight

William Price Fox
  Dixiana Moon
George Garrett
  An Evening Performance
  Do, Lord, Remember Me
  The Finished Man
Ellen Gilchrist
  The Annunciation
  *In the Land of Dreamy
    Dreams*
Marianne Gingher
  Bobby Rex's Greatest Hit
Shirley Ann Grau
  The Hard Blue Sky
  *The House on Coliseum
    Street*
  The Keepers of the House
Ben Greer
  Slammer
Barry Hannah
  The Tennis Handsome
Donald Hays
  The Dixie Association
William Humphrey
  Home from the Hill
  The Ordways
Mac Hyman
  No Time For Sergeants
Madison Jones
  A Cry of Absence
Nancy Lemann
  Lives of the Saints
  Sportsman's Paradise
Beverly Lowry
  Come Back, Lolly Ray
Valerie Martin
  A Recent Martyr
  Set in Motion
Willie Morris
  *The Last of the Southern
    Girls*
Padgett Powell
  Mrs. Hollingsworth's Men

Louis D. Rubin, Jr.
  The Golden Weather
Evelyn Scott
  The Wave
Lee Smith
  *The Last Day the Dog-
    bushes Bloomed*
Elizabeth Spencer
  The Night Travellers
  The Salt Line
  This Crooked Way
  *The Voice at the Back
    Door*
Max Steele
  Debby
Virgil Suárez
  Latin Jazz
Walter Sullivan
  The Long, Long Love
Allen Tate
  The Fathers
Peter Taylor
  *In the Miro District and
    Other Stories*
  The Widows of Thornton
Robert Penn Warren
  Band of Angels
  Brother to Dragons
  World Enough and Time
Walter White
  Flight
James Wilcox
  *Miss Undine's Living
    Room*
  North Gladiola
Joan Williams
  *The Morning and the
    Evening*
  The Wintering
Christine Wiltz
  Glass House
Thomas Wolfe
  The Hills Beyond
  The Web and the Rock